HAVE YOURSELF A MARRIED LITTLE CHRISTMAS

CLAIRE CAIN

Cover design by Jess Mastorakos - Jess@jessmastorakos.com

EBOOK: 978-1-954005-59-4

PRINT: 978-1-954005-60-0

This one's for the cat ladies. (And cat dads)

M.O.M. NETWORK

Mothers Of Military Network Message board:

SCLDG: Interesting developments around here.

JusticeLVR: Oh really? Do tell!!!!

Vic: Yes, do. Don't be coy.

SCLDG: I can't say much but it's good news. Good news!

Vic: Oh my, she's repeating herself. Must be something.

CoolyKay: Stop being so crusty, @Vic.

JusticeLVR: It's an emotional time. It's all right.

Vic: Sorry. I am happy for you @SCLDG.

SCLDG: It's alright, Vicky. Don't worry. Our job as mothers, even to our adult sons, is no small thing. I know it's been hard. I know.

Vic: Thank you.

CHAPTER ONE

Andy

Everything about this day is wrong, but I can't do anything to stop it. It's a train off the tracks and the brake is broken and the tracks are broken and... everything is broken.

You know those perfectly sunny days where your outfit is cute, and your hair cooperates, and your nails haven't chipped, and you know exactly what you're doing with your life? That perfect fall day where it's crisp but not chilly yet, the North Virginia air blessedly missing the cloying heat of summer, and the world is full of possibility?

Yeah. Today's not it. I haven't had one of those in a while, and the absence of them is downright depressing. Sun? Check. Outfit? Also, happily, check, thanks to my pumpkin patch shirt and cutest jeans with my pink Chuck Taylors. Nails and hair, check.

It's on that last one it all comes crashing down, and no

amount of positivity or laughing at the dumpster fire meme can banish the reality of the situation. Of *my* situation.

Am I actually depressed? I don't think so. But I do feel weighed down lately.

Nine months ago, my life was still on track. I was working toward opening my cat café—yes, a coffee shop with a cat adoption mission—and I was making decent progress. I'd found an investor—someone who wanted to be financially involved but not in any other way. An actual silent partner. *Perfect.*

And then I fell and broke my wrist. In public. And when I say fell, I mean I was doing a cartwheel and shanked it and it went horribly wrong. And I might've hit my head and lost consciousness for an itty-bitty minute, so a nice man on the street called emergency services and, bing, bang, boom, I got a ride in an ambulance, X-rays, a CT scan on my brain, a lovely bright pink cast on my wrist, and a bill a few weeks later that derailed all my plans.

That's what happens when you don't have insurance. And honestly, *mea culpa* here. I failed myself, but I'm feeling it well enough no one needs to lecture me. Lesson learned. But now, my bargain basement insurance isn't making a dent in the bills I'm somehow still getting from that fateful fun day, and it turns out, some labs they took popped up and made the doctor highly recommend following up with someone.

I'd put it off. I'd made it through most of my adult life without going to a primary care doctor regularly, so why should I start now?

But the concern in the nurse's voice when she called to tell me the doctor recommended that I get follow-up labs done niggled at me. As much as I am not an anxious person, I hadn't felt quite right in a while and thought maybe I should just do what she, a medical professional, suggested. But like... not right away because who confronts their fears and problems immediately?

Not it!

Plus I'm only a hair past thirty. It's far too early for words like *diagnosis* to haunt me. Granted, that's a huge privilege to even *think*, so I get it. I'd roll my eyes if someone said such a thing aloud. But in my sunny-side-up brain? Oh, yeah, the thought was there, and so was the head-in-sand reflex that said ignoring it—whatever it is—would make it go away.

I'd had my best friend Grace's real wedding—the one she and her husband planned to celebrate the fact that they wanted to stay married instead of breaking things off after their agreement for their courthouse wedding lapsed—and plenty of other things to worry about. Namely, I had to pick up as many shifts at Alex Brews as I possibly could, and even when I'm not working as manager, I take whatever shifts are left to try to pad my budget.

I'd made it through the wedding with a smile on my face and, happily, a cast-free arm by then, even if it was notably weak. But I felt worse and worse in the following weeks and finally saw the doctor a few days ago because I thought, hey, maybe this isn't all just me feeling sorry for myself about having to put off my dream for a little while thanks to a stupid broken wrist.

In my heart of hearts, I worried. And the worry dragged me down even more. And I hate fake people, but found myself amping up the "everything's fine, nothing to see here" vibes whenever I talked with Grace or my boss at the coffee shop. This triggered more feelings of guilt and *I'm a terrible friend and employee and human* spirals to the point where I could tell my cats were side-eying me more than usual.

So I went in. And they did some tests. And now, my phone is ringing, and I don't know if I can take any more bad news.

Because as I left my building this morning, I happened to check my mail and saw my landlord is raising the rent, and sure enough, my lease is up in two months.

More money I don't have. More money not going to the cat café. More time waiting on a dream I've had for as long as I can remember.

More of that tightness in my chest and pricking behind my eyes like I could dissolve into endless tears any minute and not stop despite generally not being much of a crier. I'm a glass half-full, an "it'll all work out" type. Not... whatever this feeling is.

I answer the call I've been dread-ticipating because I can't wait.

The nurse tells me they think I should come into the office.

I laugh like she cracked a joke, and I tell her I just need to know.

She says something about my parathyroid. The doctor mentioned that at my appointment, but it sounded like such a small, weird thing. What even is it?

The nurse is saying I should come in to meet with the doctor who can explain the procedure. She's saying it's a relatively minor surgery and recovery is quick. She's saying it's usually outpatient and the doctor can explain more and they can get me scheduled.

No idea if I even manage a thank you because someone has wrapped rope around my limbs, the ends pulling the tension in opposing directions so it's squeezing tight, tight, tight.

With the dread-ticipation gone, actual, sludgy, tar-like dread replaces it. It's sticky on my hands and feet and coating my throat. I'm not sure what a panic attack feels like because I'm not like this but here I am, absolutely drowning in the three p.m. October breeze.

I gasp and navigate to my web browser, quickly searching what the surgery, if I'm even remembering the name of it in my foggy state, will cost me.

My stomach drops—if possible, it falls right out of me and splats on the concrete at my feet. It's money I don't have, won't have... even if insurance helps a little—and it will only help a little—it won't make a dent.

A message flashes up, a notification from my email, and my compulsive tendency to respond immediately kicks in, overriding the shock and sadness and the feeling like I'm about to fall over the edge of an endless cliff.

But the email is a cliffside of its own. And I read, jumping, hurling myself off this additional precipice as I do.

"Situation has changed. Sorry to say we won't be able to invest due to the change in timeline."

So now my investor is gone. My debt is about to grow. I have to have surgery to fix something wrong in me, and...

And...

It's too much.

I suck in a breath, but there's no hope of a positive spin here. There's nothing to do but try to breathe, my lungs crushing as that noose tightens around me.

What will my babies do? PB and RJ will be homeless little kitties when I can't pay rent. They're too spoiled to be alley cats. They can't handle the outdoors, and RJ has seasonal allergies. His little nose will swell up, and he'll lose patches of his beautiful midnight fur. He'll be a wreck, and PB will be stressed on his behalf. He'll probably start marking and never be capable of being an indoor king again.

It's these thoughts that send me tumbling off the ledge I have valiantly tried to skirt with my sunny-side up spin for the last few months.

No point in trying to hold it off any longer. I crouch right here in the alleyway outside work, bury my face in my legs, and sob my guts out.

CHAPTER TWO

Gruff

I stop dead in the street when I see her.

I've never seen this woman with anything less than a beaming smile on her face save the scowls she gives me. She's the persistent dandelions that burst out of the grass before anything else considers blooming. And a weed is an apt metaphor for her because she's so preposterously bright-eyed, it feels like an angel had to lose its halo just to supply her glow.

But this... this isn't right.

Instead of sending me an eyeroll and mocking grin at the counter when I order my black coffee and she pretends I've ordered some travesty like a caramel double whip extra sugar sprinkles triple syrup Frappuccino when she repeats back my order, she's hunched in a ball outside the coffee shop, head tucked into her knees.

She's a little hedgehog curled around herself.

Normally a fair bit shorter than me in real life, and maybe even petite, right now she's tucked into a little shell doing her best impression of a medium-sized dog napping, though there's nothing restful about her pose or the grief wracking her.

I wouldn't even recognize her like this if it weren't for the pink tips of her braid and the reality that something in me would recognize her in a dark, crowded room or in costume or if she cut off those bright ends. Not the point, so I move to address her when, normally, I would actively *not* be the one to initiate.

"Hey, Andy. Whoa." My voice comes out rough with urgency, the clear sense something is wrong broadcasting in every cell of my body. "What's going on? What's wrong?"

She's sobbing, shoulders shaking, and her arms are wrapped tightly around her, back against the wall. She's a little egg nestled in this alleyway and she's cracking.

I crouch, daring to set a hand on her shoulder in case she hasn't heard me. She lifts her head slowly, her mascara blackening the skin around her eyes, so she looks truly miserable. Her face is splotchy and red, her usually perfect skin a tear-stained mess. Her pert nose and distractingly pink lips don't distract me today—not when she's wincing against whatever it is hurting her. When her gaze connects with mine, my heart squeezes because I recognize the pain there. I've felt something like this before—I can't find the right words, but my gut knows I have.

It is... uncomfortable. I don't feel hearty things very often, and this particular person elicits only mild annoyance and other responses I choose not to dwell on. But this is not our usual interaction and so, there it is.

"I—I can't do this. I don't know how to do this."

Her voice is ragged and broken, and I've never seen anything like it.

I can't stand it, her grief and pain, and without a single thought, I know I'll do whatever I can to make this better. We've never gotten along, never been friends, never connected, but the wrongness of her like this gives me a mission.

I tend to be an all-or-nothing person, and my effort to serve my country and do something good has been in my work in the military. Nothing could've prepared me for the vast seas of gray in this life, but in this moment, it is all black and white. Andy shouldn't be in this situation and I will do anything to stop it.

Anything.

It's desperation and imperative. It's a fully blown operation, no briefings or power points needed.

"What? What is it? Are you hurt? Are you in pain?" I rub my thumb over the skin of her upper arm where I'm touching her, hoping for comfort in the small gesture despite the foreignness of the contact between us, and for me, at all.

Her eyes shut in misery. "I just got diagnosed with—" she says something I don't quite make out because it's garbled by a sob. "And that's not so bad. It's fixable. But I am so—"

She slaps a hand over her mouth, and her eyes are wide, almost fearful, when she looks at me.

"What? Just tell me. Just say whatever it is, and we'll fix it." I feel certain if she'll just tell me, I'll move mountains to make this stop. I suspect, knowing who Andy is, that there is no gray area here. I'll become Atlas and carry the world for her or find a radioactive spider and Spiderman myself into a solution. There has to be one.

She shakes her head, then shifts and lets her legs stretch out in front of her, finally seating herself on the ground. "This is my problem. I can't tell you, and I especially can't tell *you*."

"Why not? Who would I tell?" It's a false argument, and she knows it.

"JJ? Grace? Your doorman at whatever fancy building you live in in the city?" Her head falls back against the brick wall, and she gazes up at the sky.

Not bothering to correct her assumption about where I live, I press a little. "I swear I will not say a word to anyone."

She swallows, her throat working, and a sheen covers her eyes. I brace, resisting the flip of panic that hits my gut because she's going to cry again, and I don't know how long to stay here with her if she won't talk.

But like she often does, Andy surprises me. Her gaze shifts to mine and a tear does track down her cheek, but she isn't sobbing. She's cradling her right wrist, tucking it to her chest.

In a steady voice, she says, "I'm in debt. Like, crazy amounts of debt, thanks to some medical issues I've had. And that has cascaded enough that I've had to put my plans for my business on hold. That's not new, but I was hoping—"

She firms her chin, her lips an underline to the misery of her face, and clears her throat. "I've been working more, trying to pay it off. But I just got word that my rent is increasing, my investor pulled out so I'm that much farther from my goal for the café, and I need surgery in order to address the problem and get better, which will cost me a cool 10k at least. So." Her lips tremble. "Yeah."

I blink. I'm blissfully ignorant when it comes to medical costs. I've been in the military over twenty years and haven't paid a dime for any medical needs *ever*. I've been lucky enough to have few issues, but I recognize the benefit I carry.

"I wish I could just... give you my insurance." It's a ridiculous thing to say, but I'm not sure I've ever felt something more distinctly than the desire to do exactly that.

She lets out a little laugh. "Me, too."

It wouldn't solve all her problems, but it would help with the surgery. I want to ask what the diagnosis is, and understand exactly what she needs, but I don't want to take us back there.

"You are forbidden to tell anyone because I refuse to encroach on their little honeymoon phase." There's a spark of her usual determination and fire in her eye now.

"I would never. Though I will point out their honeymoon phase has to be long over." They've been married for nearly nine months.

There comes a sly grin, a little glimpse of the woman I know.

"I feel bad for you if you think that's true. I know we have different worldviews, but really, man? They've only been really married for, what? Six weeks?"

I nod, humorless. That's all I am to her, most likely, but I can't summon any cheer when my mind is running through the ways I could help her, and my chest is tight with the memory that even six weeks into my own marriage, something had been off.

Years have passed since the dawning of that marriage, and since the end of it. Why it should jab at me now, I don't know, but Andy doesn't seem to have noticed, or she just assumes I'm being me.

"Whatever. Anyway, don't mention this. Please."

There's that pleading in her voice again, and I move instantly to reassure her.

"Of course I won't."

She swallows again, dipping her chin. "Well. Thanks. And... thanks for not mentioning this ever again. It'll be fine." She exhales slowly and her eyes find the sky again.

Those eyes...

"Hope the day improves for you," I say, because I need to get out of here. I need to think.

"Thanks. Have a good one."

She pushes herself up to standing, and I resist the urge to offer her a hand. Natural instinct tells me touching her won't do me any good.

I leave, bypassing the coffee shop and heading to my car. I'm oddly numb on the outside, but inside, I feel... tossed. Like a ship on a stormy sea, and Andy's the one making the waves. I have a gnawing need to make things better for her despite having next to no relationship with her.

My gut and heart are twisted into a knot, and I wish I could get her back to that version of her, the one I glimpsed for only seconds, the one that sends my pulse notching higher with frustration and exasperation. Not worry or an anxious imperative to solve her problem.

Finally, I arrive at work, which used to feel like a sanctuary but now mostly feels like something I do because I don't know what else to do. Twenty-plus years in a career can teach a man many things, and I don't know many whose views don't change along the way. My altruism did, to some degree, but that innate need to solve, to right, to make better... it's there. It's still here. And there's already a wild, utterly impossible but potentially perfect, idea hatching.

CHAPTER THREE

Gruff

My mother is, as always, impeccably dressed.

Ever the politician's wife, even in retirement for the both of them, she is polished in her navy slacks, blouse, and a jacket she likely checked at the door, but always with a calculating glint to her eyes.

"You look tired, son. Everything okay?" She stirs a tiny spoon in her delicate china teacup. She's invited me to her favorite swanky DC hotel complete with renowned restaurant like she does once a month, insisting we take high tea like tourists instead of simply having lunch like normal people do.

"I haven't been sleeping very well," I admit before I think better of it.

Now I've done it—might as well have slit a wrist dangling off a boatside near a shiver of sharks.

Eloise Gruff's gaze narrows, but in the fiction of my mind, I see her pupils blow wide, ready to feast.

"And why not?"

I buy myself a minute to formulate the thought, unsure if I want to say anything at all. But I've been thinking... can't *stop* thinking, really, about Andy. About the red rimming her bright blue eyes and the desperation in her voice. About how wrong it felt to see her not just upset but truly downtrodden.

"I've had a lot on my mind." There. That'll—

"Wilson James Gruff, if you're going to be vague, why even agree to see me?"

I cough, never actually surprised by her bluntness and demanding way, but always kind of... well, somehow always still a little surprised.

"My apologies. I'm just... not sure how to explain. I have a..." What would I call Andy? A person I know via mutual friends? A woman who was the maid of honor to my best man at our friends' wedding a few months ago? I land on, "...friend. She's in trouble. And I want to help her."

The gleam in my mother's eye brightens.

"And can you? Help her?"

My pulse jumps and my heart churns with an inkling of a plan I will not mention to her. "I don't know."

Her brows pull up. "I imagine you can. You're resourceful. Creative, even, when you choose to be."

I don't respond.

She sniffs and lifts her teacup off its saucer an inch. "My son. If you feel you can help this person, then you must. You've resources and privileges aplenty, so do whatever you can. Lend a hand in any way you see fit."

I'm struck by this—her effusive, almost imploring

speech. But she's right. I should help if I can, and I will. I only need to figure out how.

For now, we'll move on. "Thank you. I'll do my best. Enough about that for now, though. Tell me about you."

She graciously accepts my subject change. "I'm already working on holiday plans." Her brightness stutters for a heartbeat. "I've been wanting to tell you that your brother is coming back."

The wheels spinning in my head, working to find a solution for Andy, grind to a halt. "Back."

She nods, a tight semblance of a smile at the corners of her mouth. "Yes."

"For Christmas." It's not a question. He has occasionally done this in the past. As part of the diplomatic staff at the US Embassy in Korea, he's nestled happily abroad and has been for well over half a decade. Having a few continents and oceans between us is for the best.

My mother's expression shifts to one I think of as her Senator's Wife Face. It's convincingly natural, but I know the pull at her lips is false and the set of her eyes is studiously warm without a hint of being practiced.

"Yes, for Christmas. We'll do it at the house here in DC, keep it simple." Her gaze softens and she sighs. "You'll come, won't you?"

I hear it. The hope there.

I'm a forty-two-year-old man, and I still want to make my mother happy. I want her approval even, and worse, I want my father's. I'm a colonel in the US Army, a rank I've worked for over twenty years to achieve, and one that few people ever come close to, let alone at this age, and yet I feel small in this moment, thinking about my brother.

My younger brother.

My neck itches and I'm hot. My collar's too tight, and I

wish I didn't have to sit up so straight because I'm instantly tired now that we've broached the subject of Jason, and I just want to lay down and take a nap.

It's not something I'm proud of, but it's honest. And she knows this is hard for me. Having him here will be brutal, especially if I spend the holiday watching him with his wife—the thought grates down my throat, leaving me raw—while I'm sitting there alone.

I've been just fine alone. But staying at my house in Alexandria when the rest of them are together would be worse, and so I tell her the truth.

"Of course I'll be there. Nothing could keep me away."

Not even my little brother returning to grace us all with his inimitable presence and knowing how I'll hate every minute. Not the dread I feel for sharing the same air as him and my father at the same time. Not... any of it.

But what I will do... the idea is formulating, and the knot in my gut is telling me I must act. No more sitting around and embracing this place in life and letting inertia win.

It's time to turn the tables.

CHAPTER FOUR

Andy

If someone had told me I'd be waiting for Colonel Gruff to grace me with his presence on a Saturday evening on King Street in Old Town, Alexandria, I would've laughed in their face.

But when I got his text yesterday, that was enough of a surprise. Grace had messaged to ask if she could give him my number. She had to be suspicious about why he'd want it, and I shared the sentiment.

Gruff and I had miraculously managed not to exchange numbers in the course of our maid of honor and best man duties during the wedding last summer, primarily because Grace and JJ were so involved and left very little for us to manage.

If he'd told her about our encounter earlier this week, she would've launched into a diatribe about my being sick and not asking for help, so I believe he hadn't.

And therefore, I was extremely curious as to what he had to say.

Now? Even more so.

The restaurant I'm sitting in has lots of natural wood coloring with dark metal accents and a huge mirror behind a sprawling bar. There are high top tables in the official bar area, and standard tables in spokes leading from the center-piece. I've walked by here a handful of times but never felt fancy enough to come in—not that it's formal, but it's not really my style.

And with the recent adjustments to my budget, the subcategory of "fun money" is non-existent. I do have an allotment for guacamole and margaritas because a girl's gotta live, but it's whittled down to once monthly, and I feel it in my soul.

I continue to appreciate the chic vibes as I sit at the bar, my ice water resting on a cardboard coaster atop the polished wood of the bar. I could really go for a margarita about now, but something tells me I'll be wise to maintain complete clarity going into... whatever this is.

The front door of the entrance swings open, and I glance that way when the cool breeze from the crisp late-October air swirls in with a tall man in jeans and a black sweater on top.

My stomach flips when I realize it's him.

I have never pretended to think he's unattractive. Only a fool would do that. The man is tall, dark, and handsome, and of course frowning. His serious face comes toward me with his usual direct approach that simultaneously disarms me and makes me feel all fluttery. His widow's peak gives him a dashing, almost villainous vibe, especially with his dark hair. There's more gray at his temples and the sides of his head, I notice, but inevitably this does nothing but make him hotter.

Honestly, men. They have no idea how good they have it.

"Thank you for meeting me. May I?" He nods to the seat at his left as though I haven't been sitting here waiting for him.

"Of course."

The bartender must've seen him walk in because he's there, hovering, as Gruff sits.

"Whatever IPA's on tap. Thanks," Gruff orders, then shifts his gaze to me, expectant.

"Uh, I'll have a... sparkling wine? Something not too sweet?" I ask, as though it's a question and not a statement about what I want.

Why am I like this?

The bartender nods and gets to work while I take a long sip of my water. My mouth has gone dry and I'm fidgety. I have no idea what he wants, but if he doesn't start talking soon, I'm probably going to verbally spew every thought in my head without context or warning as sometimes happens when I'm wound up and exhausted at the same time.

"I have a proposal. I'd like to ask you to consider it for a few days before you give me an answer. I'm hoping it's something we can both benefit from."

His tone is so serious, it sends a little rush of nervousness through me. He's normally crusty and generally unpleasant, so I'm not sure what I'm supposed to do with this next-level version of that.

Granted, he wasn't unpleasant when I was blubbering about my diagnosis and needing surgery and all my dreams getting farther and farther out of reach. He was kind. And he appears to have kept his word regarding not telling Grace or JJ.

Even if he'd been awful, I would be here to see what he had to say. I'm too curious a person to *not* show up, even if it's someone I, by all accounts, dislike.

"I'm listening." I mentally pat myself on the back for keeping my response simple and not launching into a thousand preemptive questions like ninety-percent of my brain is begging to do.

He pauses a moment, his blue eyes a startlingly light color in this dimly lit part of the restaurant.

"A few questions first. When will you need surgery?"

I swallow hard. Normally, I resist talking about any of my fun medical revelations because no one needs to be burdened with my baggage, but he saw me bawling over them, so why *not* tell him?

"I can't schedule it until I can figure out how to pay for it or talk with the hospital about a payment plan..." I exhale, the pressure in my chest spiking uncomfortably. "I haven't talked with them again since the last time I saw you."

It's only been a few days, so I don't feel bad about this. I'm not exactly avoiding the problem, I just don't have any real solution. My usual hard work and positivity have failed me so miserably the last nine months, it's hard to properly quantify. No, I will not allow my cats to become homeless, but yes, I have given myself permission to internally wallow while praying a miracle comes along and gives me a ride on the debt-free, lower rent, new investor rainbow.

And if he's going to judge me for it, maybe I won't stay to hear him out.

He absorbs my response, a small nod the only real indication he's heard me. The bartender delivers our drinks, settling Gruff's bright foamy beer on a coaster next to where he places my flute of bubbling pale-golden wine. He's gone, sliding down to the other end of the bar, before either of us says thank you.

Gruff's large hand wraps around his glass so I pinch the stem of my drink and we both take sips. I'm eying him as though if I look away he'll lash out and… what? Steal my wallet? The man undoubtedly has more money than I do, so I have no idea what I'm wary of. Maybe just that he seems to have something he wants to say, but is also avoiding saying it.

"So? The proposal you want me to carefully consider for a matter of days… did you want to actually tell me? Or am I supposed to guess?" I sound like a snot, but I've lost my patience now that he's got me thinking about surgery and medical debt and all of those fun things that have nothing to do with fall vibes and handsome men and curiosity.

He takes another sip of his beer, then angles himself toward me. His knee brushes the side of my leg, then moves away again.

"I've been thinking about your situation—about how you need insurance. I have good insurance that could help."

I blink. "Um, yeah. I can't exactly join the Army to get insurance. Fun thought, but I'm more of a pacifist, if I had to categorize myself. I—"

"I don't mean you should join the Army. That's absurd."

My brows raise at that. "Absurd? I could hack it, if that's what you're insinuating. Especially if I didn't have a jacked up parathyroid trying to—"

He huffs, shakes his head, and plants his hand in the space between us on the bar. "We should get married. That's what I'm saying."

CHAPTER FIVE

Gruff

Her pretty blue eyes stare unblinking at me.

"Um... I don't know you. I don't even know your first name." She grips her glass in a fist and slugs down several large gulps.

"You've known me for nearly a year," I counter.

"Technically, sure. But it's not like we've been friends. We've interacted as friends of friends, kind of, and my first point still stands—*I don't even know your first name.*"

She's gesticulating enough I can tell I've really thrown her with this suggestion.

I catch her gaze and wait for a beat, then tell her, "Wilson."

She huffs and mumbles something under her breath.

"What?"

When she looks up, she appears almost angry. "I said, of course it's something adorable."

This is unexpected and, oddly, does something to me. I can't describe what, other than it's similar to finishing a beer on an empty stomach. I'm a little... floaty, for lack of a better term, and I'm honestly not sure what to do with it. I've always felt Wilson is a bit dorky, or maybe I've had one too many people, including my ex-wife, crack jokes to that effect. *Adorable* is unexpected.

Also not the point here.

So, I power ahead.

"Let me explain my suggestion. If we marry, you will instantly have insurance through Tricare. You could move ahead with any medical procedures with virtually no cost... I did a little research, and it appears the out-of-pocket cap is a thousand dollars in one year, so it would be that or less, for whatever you need."

Her mouth drops open. "Um. Wow. That's incredible. But, again, I don't know you well enough for this, and we haven't dated, and isn't that insurance fraud? Or something? Something fraud-y?"

I want to smile at *fraud-y* but I don't because I can tell she'll be annoyed if I do that. This is the version of Andy I'm used to—off-kilter in a way I like but have never and won't ever admit aloud I do. Also, not the point. What I really need from her is to hear me, think about this seriously, and say yes.

"It wouldn't be fraud. I've looked into it." Sure, there's some risk the military could discover our situation and be angry about it, but it's hard to prove. Even with the little contract I drew up as evidence, we can easily get around it. Or so I think. I haven't consulted JJ on this yet and I don't think I'm going to until the last possible minute, otherwise I might find myself wussing out.

"Okay. Okay. Yeah. Okay..." She's talking fast and wringing her hands in her lap.

Not good.

"It would be. Okay. And you could get out of your lease, save on rent, and move in with me. I have two bedrooms, you have one, your own bathroom... it'd be fine. We'd be roommates for all intents and purposes, until we... aren't."

Her eyes widen so big, I can tell she's jumped to a very nasty conclusion.

"Are you seriously suggesting I pay you back in—"

"No. No." I've unconsciously set a hand on her wrist and when I realize, right as she looks down to stare at the evidence of my impertinence, I pull it back. "I mean, I'd get something out of it, too, and it would not be sleeping with you."

Would I mind? No. Andy is a ridiculously beautiful woman, and I haven't attempted to deny this truth, even the first time I saw her and instantly recognized her dislike of me. But no, that would not be part of the arrangement.

I would consider making that sacrifice if she insisted, but—

Shaking my head, I stop the inane thought. That really isn't part of the deal here.

Since she hasn't said anything, I rush in to give more information. "I'm sure you're wondering why I'd do this. I have my own reasons. I have a family situation and I'd like to..." I haven't figured out how to word this in a way that doesn't seem completely pathetic.

While my mind is flipping through options to phrase how I'd benefit, she interjects.

"I really need you to complete your sentence because my teen years were spent watching movies like *Pretty Woman* on repeat and I am really not prepared to be your sexy Hollywood Boulevard escort. Though I could totally rock the 'Big mistake. Huge.' moment if we want to arrange that."

I have... no idea what she's talking about. She must read this on my face.

She presses her lips together and I notice her cheeks are faintly rosy. It's more than a little endearing hearing her ramble on nervously. I wish I could enjoy it—let myself be charmed by it, since for once, she's not simply insulting my scowling manner. But I can't enjoy her because my sludgy, mildly humiliated brain is still working up the courage to admit why I'm even considering this.

"No escort... well, not in the, uh, intimate sense. But I do need a wife. In the purely on paper sense, except for the holidays. I'll be with family and—" I clear my throat, hoping the froggy strain there will dissipate. "And I need to be married when I'm there."

She tilts her head a little, like she's thinking this over and not sure what it means. I haven't been clear, but I don't have it in me to explain all the details.

"So, no physical stuff. Just Mrs. Wilson Gruff by your side for presents and boiled goose?"

I bark an odd laugh that makes her grin.

"Boiled goose?" I ask, because where does she get this stuff?

She waves it away. "If you're serious about this, I'm interested."

She swallows, nods to herself, and is about to say something else, but I interrupt before she can do what I think she's going to do.

"I'm glad you're considering it. Please keep thinking it over. I have a contract I'll send you via e-mail. This way, there's no confusion. You can have JJ look at it, or—"

"I still don't want anyone to know about... anything." Her gaze drops to her hands, and I resist the urge to growl my frustration with her.

"You'll have to tell them when we're married. We'll need witnesses, and don't you think they'll understand, considering they did the same thing less than a year ago?"

JJ and Grace's marriage was for practical reasons, just like this. Granted, I gave him trouble for it, and he was his usual workaholic, thick-headed self when it came to realizing he was madly in love with Grace, but when he did... it's what everyone dreams of.

And even if it's not how my story went, I'm glad it's how theirs did.

"Don't I recall you saying something about not ever marrying again?" she asks after finishing the last drops of her champagne or whatever the bartender gave her.

I think back, not remembering specifically, but it does sound like me. "I never intended to. But this is different. No feelings, no fuss. It's a business deal, if I were the kind of person who made those. And it's good for both of us."

Andy is objectively attractive and charming in a way I admire but can't really access, so feelings won't enter into it. I'm not sure I even know how to have them—my ex-wife would certainly corroborate the likelihood I'm incapable.

So. All clear there.

Even if I do feel a draw toward her—maybe look a little too long at the slope of her neck or the curve of her chin or the pretty way she purses her lips ever so slightly when she swallows.

She's squinting at me, trying to understand, most likely. Good luck to her, because I don't fully understand myself.

What I do know is I can't go to my parents' house unattached. I need someone there, someone I can put my arm around and call my own so the pity doesn't cause us all to bleed out on the lovely hand-woven rugs in their opulent living room.

As though she can feel the hint of desperation shining through my thoughts, she stands and extends her hand.

I'm still taller than her sitting on this barstool, so I stand, too, even though I tower over her like this.

I take her hand.

It feels like a gut punch when our palms slip together, when our fingers clasp and we shake once, twice. It must be thanks to the gravity of her being open to the idea I've presented.

She lets go and my heart is hammering.

"Well, Wilson. I'll sleep on it just to be sure, but I'm pretty sure you have a deal," she says with a smile.

She slides out the door and I gaze after her, pulse still running, wondering if it's really all as simple as I've made it seem.

Must be the adrenaline.

—————

CHAPTER SIX

Andy

I never dreamed about the white dress. No, not little Andy, nerd alert of all sunny little nerds.

I dreamed about the cats.

Yes, childhood Andy's wedding included cats in many of the roles. Mind you, she imagined a human groom of amorphous appearance, but flower girl?

No, ma'am, flower cat.

Ring bearer?

Pshaw. Ring *cat*.

Wedding party?

Obviously enough, wedding cats.

At this point, anyone can guess that instead of a bouquet, it's a basket of kittens. And no, this is not practical but who said anything about that?

Perhaps I wasn't really dreaming about a wedding, but

simply allowing my mind to enjoy the many funny feline substitutes in a wedding line-up. I was seven, maybe younger, after all. And I'd never had a cat, so I spent my time dreaming of them.

I never stopped. Maybe that's why I've dreamed more about cats than I have about husbands.

Also probably why I'm not more of a mess today, even though PB and RJ are not present to act as my flower boys.

"You're really doing this?" Grace asks, concern knitting her brows together in the middle.

I gaze at my reflection, wondering if the dress is right.

Or wrong?

Or maybe I'm really wondering if all of this is right. *Am I really marrying a man I hardly know just for the health insurance?* Based on my current location and getup and the very fine job I did with my cat eye liner, yes, I am.

Maybe I should be second-guessing, but I'm not. There's something about Gruff that makes me feel confident in him and in this whole set-up. He's not hitting on me or manipulating me, and he is literally solving my problem. Yes, it's unconventional, but people have done far wilder things to meet their basic human needs.

I can do this and get what I need. He'll get whatever it is he does, which I assume will eventually become clearer than *I need a wife for a week*, and someday I'll look back on this and marvel at how freaking daring I was. I mean, this is ultimate girl boss territory, right? This is taking me closer to health and therefore closer to making my dreams a reality.

Okay, maybe it's not all that girl-bossy, but it's self-care-y, at least. We'll go with that buzzword. And my dress, whether right or wrong, is really, *really* pretty.

It looks good, I'll admit. It's a boat neck that splays wide on my shoulders, skimming the edge of my collar bones with three-quarters sleeves and a fairly full skirt. I can't remember what it's called, but when I twirled around in the store, it flared out so prettily, I was sold. And by sold, I mean *borrowed*, God bless the woman for doing me the huge favor. There is no world in which I could afford to own this dress, especially right now.

It's also blush pink instead of white. A perfect piece of me for the day. I love how the bright pink ends of my hair rest against the pale blush fabric below my shoulders, the rest of my golden blond waves a nice contrast. All in all it feels less stodgy, though I'm fairly certain Gruff has never dated let alone considered marrying a woman with any amount of pink hair. Ah well, such is the oddity of a situation like this, and all the more why I'm happy to feel good in my skin—or, my outfit—today.

"I am. It'll be fine. *Great* even," I say, smiling at my reflection and willing it into existence. Granted, all those cat wedding plans failed me, so maybe this will, too.

But, no. This will work out just fine.

It's temporary—six months, or maybe even less, of my life is a drop in the bucket. It's until I'm fully recovered. Our agreement is clear. And honestly, I have no other options.

"I thought you hated him, though." Grace sounds as baffled as she should.

It's weird, this thing I'm doing.

"I don't *hate* him. I just find his general demeanor and approach to life off-putting." *Not true*, my brain yells at me. But it's easier to pretend everything between me and him is like that and not more complicated after seeing his human side.

And after he came up with this whole idea that is, in no small way, changing my life.

And, you know, the hot side. The man who showed up at the bar and made that proposal? Glory hallelujah. I had to tamp down my googly eyes bugging out at him because the whole collared shirt, five o'clock shadow, gruff Gruff look was delicious. And that's not to mention the hum I kept feeling bouncing between us that made *no* sense.

I didn't even look at him straight on when I saw him a few minutes ago, before I ducked into the bathroom because his uniform is stupid-hot. It's just all... it's dangerous. Because he's more than attractive to me and this element is unhelpful, too. Somehow, the more human he gets, the hotter, and we need to keep that business locked up tight.

Grace cackles. "Oh, is that all?"

I shrug a shoulder. "He's got what I need. And I can... help him with what he needs."

"I bet you can," she says, wiggling her brows.

I groan and shake my head, but heat creeps into my cheeks. I've made my peace with the unconventional nature of what I'm about to do. Grace, of all people, should get it. She married a man out of necessity right around this time last year. They were childhood friends, and their families knew each other, so it wasn't quite the same set-up I currently march toward in my gorgeous blush heels, but still.

It's not unheard of in life to do a thing because you need to.

"You know what I mean," I say, anxious this is all a lot more sordid than I agreed to, even though he looked me in the eye and said he wasn't planning to sleep with me.

Her arms wrap around my shoulders, and she squeezes, both of us looking at our reflection in the bathroom mirror.

"I do. Trust me, if anyone on Earth gets what you're doing, I do. I just wish you'd told me what was going on."

I deflate. "I'm sorry. You were happy and loving life and busy and I..." Clearing my throat, I say the words even if I hate them. "I didn't want to be a burden."

Grace's eyes see all the way through me. But she has mercy on me and smiles softly. "You will never be a burden, my friend. But I also want to say I'm not here to talk you out of this. So if you're sure, then let's do this thing."

I chuckle, the sound oddly watery considering how sure I really am. I'm certain this is the only way I can make things work—the only way I can ever get my hands on what I really want. A café of my own, my little dream materialized. It keeps me, and especially the cats, from becoming homeless. And not that I would ever ask my parents for help, but it keeps them from ever even knowing I've had a problem. Saying I hate to be a burden is an understatement, especially when it comes to them.

I took the twenty-four hours Gruff had asked me to, and then I texted him. We've gone back and forth about a few more things—he sent me the contract via e-mail, and then he's been gone. Literally, out of the country on a temporary... I've forgotten what the acronym is, but he was gone. So I haven't seen him or hardly talked to him other than to confirm we were inviting JJ and Grace and that yes, we were still doing this.

Nerves light me up from the inside, but not in a purely foreboding way. Still in that *this changes everything* kind of way. And... duh.

Obviously.

Not only does it change my marital status, it'll also change my mailing address and my health insurance situation.

Thank goodness.

And nothing else.

"I'm sure. And—" I smooth my hands down the satin of my dress and take a huge breath. "I'm ready."

Grace grins. "Alright, then. Let's go get you hitched to Colonel Gruff!"

CHAPTER SEVEN

Gruff

Marriage is for men who need.

Companionship. Someone to take care of them. Someone to care for. Sex. Maybe partnership could be differentiated from companionship, if one really minces hairs.

I need none of it. Sex would be nice, sure, though that doesn't necessarily require marriage, but my point stands.

I've done it before, given it a shot, and I know very well I'm not the marrying kind anymore.

Because of this, it should strike me as the greatest of ironies that I now stand in my service uniform facing a woman in a wedding dress while she's saying the words, "I do."

And I'm saying them back.

And the nice old man, the same one I recall adjudicating—is that the word?—Grace and JJ's wedding almost exactly a year ago, is saying, "...the state of Virginia, I pronounce you married."

No husband and wife business, which is just as well.

I have no intention of being a husband to this woman, just like I'm certain she has no desire to be my wife.

Except in the contractually agreed upon function while interacting with my family.

This is an agreement, and we're on the same page with it. I know this because there are pages to our contract, the thing we signed digitally weeks ago when we finalized all of this. And the only reason I'm standing here.

Whatever I like about Andy, that's all moot. I'm doing this for me, so I don't have to drag into the Gruff family Christmas single and weighed down by the way my brother manages to be all the things I'm not, and so Andy isn't bankrupted by having a simple surgery that will change her overall health.

Simple.

Do I dwell on how the slight pink tint to her dress doesn't bother me? And how her pale, smooth skin lit with warmth intrigues me? Or the way, when I get close enough to catch a hint of her minty, sweet scent, my stomach clenches?

Or the truth that she looks so easygoing, so certain, I'm also set at ease. She generally does the opposite—weasels her way under my skin with a raised brow or a sly little remark, then stays there, a splinter burrowing deeper, relentless.

I'm as comfortable physically as I am any other day. I'm in my "pinks and greens" service uniform and it cuts a nice figure, plus the blush of Andy's dress actually looks great with my World War II-inspired modern uniform. Works out well that I needed to be wearing this for a meeting I have next, which seemed like a perfectly normal thing to schedule after a ceremony to a woman I only kind of know.

But today, she's so clear-eyed and her cheeks have a little tint to them that makes her unignorably beautiful. I should be finding the half-inch of pink at the bottom of her long, honey blond hair a sign of her immaturity, evidence she is so far from right for me that this is all a mistake, and yet it's not. Because she's not supposed to be right for me any more than I am for her, and that, too, makes this closer to something right in itself.

The chemistry I felt tucked into the spaces between us at the bar a month ago when I proposed this arrangement still hovers around me. Did she feel it?

Does she feel the electric current zipping between us when our eyes meet? Does her center of gravity shift toward me like mine does toward her, like my orbit, my entire elemental being has changed in some way now that we've done this thing?

Good grief. The long night and lack of sleep has caught up with me and sent me into dramatics.

"Congratulations!" Grace says, throwing her arms around Andy as we all make our way out of the small courtroom and into the echoing stone entryway of the courthouse.

Andy chuckles, a sound that feels like a small jab to my ribs. I haven't seen her since the night I suggested we do this. I wish we'd gotten a drink last night, or had a conversation before the ceremony. All we had time for was a quick, "You okay?" and her nod.

JJ extends his hand and I take it. We shake, and then pull each other in, a quick pat on the back before releasing.

"Congrats."

He knows me as well as most anyone, which isn't to say

all that much, though we've gotten fairly close in the last year. Ever since I attended his civil ceremony at this very place, and he began his sham of a wedding, which then evolved into something real.

Based on the way he and Grace lace fingers and how she leans into him, resting her head on his shoulder for a moment before sending him a little wink that makes me feel like I shouldn't have seen it, they're doing as well as they have been the last few months.

"Thanks for being here," I say, because I do appreciate it. Even if I'm a little befuddled, a little embarrassed, and more than a little nervous about this new development.

"Of course. I can't wait to watch this unfold," JJ says, a grin on the quiet man's face speaking louder than I've ever heard him.

I grumble, because what would I say to that?

"You guys getting lunch? Or, what's the plan?" Grace asks, gaze switching between us.

For the first time since she said, "I do," Andy looks at me. I catch... something there, and almost regret having to say, "No. I've got a two o'clock briefing at the Pentagon."

JJ and Grace share a look I can't decipher, and Andy nods. "We've done the deed, so now we're off in separate directions."

Her bright blue eyes slide to meet mine, and *she* winks at *me*.

She winked at me.

My brain flatlines.

I cannot for the life of me remember a socially appropriate response. *Any* response.

What is words?

And why did a wink from a woman I barely know but

am now married to make me feel so completely like I've fallen on my head?

"Right, Wilson?" Andy asks, a quizzical expression making her lips tilt in a charming smile even as her eyes search my face.

I cough, my mind jumpstarted by her saying my name. "Right. Yes. So. Until later."

And that's it. I nod to Grace and JJ, turn on my heel, and leave, reminding myself that ultimately, nothing has changed.

M.O.M. NETWORK

Mothers Of Military Network Message board:

SCLDG: It's done! My sources tell me they're married. I am elated.

Vic: I honestly don't know anyone else who would type out the word elated in a messaging app.

JusticeLVR: Haha, too true @Vic. And yay! Congratulations! A new daughter-in-law.

CoolyKay: Wonderful news. Thrilled for you. When will you meet her? I take it you weren't there for the ceremony?

SCLDG: Sadly, no, but if all goes to plan maybe we'll manage a real coup like @JustiveLVR and have a summer wedding to celebrate the success. I don't want to nose in before they've made a real connection.

Vic: That's the goal, I suppose.

JusticeLVR: I can say it's been lovely for me, but I know it may not go that way for everyone. Even so, crossing fingers and saying prayers those two end up the same way.

CoolyKay: We'll all hope so.

SCLDG: They'll come for Christmas. There may be some challenges there, but I suspect those very things will be precisely what brings them together.

Vic: Keep us posted.

JusticeLVR: Yes please.

CHAPTER EIGHT

Andy

G ruff's house is more charming than any single man's home has a right to be.

Scratch that. Married man.

Married to *me*.

Weird!

Weirder, I'm moving into his house sight unseen and without him here. Well, actually, I packed up everything I'm moving in here, and he insisted on paying movers to deliver to his house while we were busy, y'know, gettin' hitched. I have the code to his alarm and the key he slipped me after the ceremony and, voilà. He'll come home tonight, and we'll be living together. Roommates. Cohabitants.

I have resorted to making these lists of synonyms to help me process the reality that I am now married to Wilson James Gruff and it is wild.

Also, his first name is *Wilson*. I've been marveling at this for the last month since he told me, and I still can't move past it.

The man is gigantic and grumpy and dark and stupid levels of handsome, and he is now my husband, and his first name is Wilson.

I need all the information about this fact. Family name? Famous reference? Historical influence? Pity he's technically too old to have been named after Tom Hanks' beloved beachball in *Castaway*. Would've been neat.

Also, can I call him Will? Son seems inappropriate as a nickname, right?

There's something soft and almost sweet about the name Wilson. Don't ask me why, but I keep giggling about being married to Wilson Gruff as I slide my hands across the marble countertops of his kitchen and peek inside the immaculate blue cabinets to find crisp white dishes in neat stacks.

And yes, the cabinets are a dusky Baltic blue. White and gray marbling on the counters and a chevron-style stone backsplash. A huge sink. None of it black, like I might've imagined once or twice in the last few weeks while mentally preparing to move into a house I'd never seen.

Does this man cook, or is he just so wealthy that only the best will do? Stainless steel appliances sit flush with the cabinetry, of course, but none of it is out of place in this historic, almost cozy-feeling place.

But it's the living room that kills me—straight up paralyzes my heart with its beauty.

Twelve-foot ceilings and nearly as large windows with arching tops and floor-length gauzy drapes. A cream-colored deep sectional couch with giant throw pillows, ridiculously soft-looking blankets at the far ends, and a little tray sitting on the coffee table that gives me ideas for what I want to do with the corner spot.

It's all facing a gorgeous fireplace that is better than any TV I've seen center a room. In fact, I don't even see a TV in here, which is curious, but maybe he watches in his room? There's just a huge painting hung above the mantel.

This jumpstarts me into action, not wanting to linger for too long or I'll be lulled into the couch and never leave. I head down the hall, ignoring the room with the door closed because he said that's his room and I won't start this whole fake married slumber party situation by invading his space even more than I already am.

PB meows—for as outgoing as he tends to be, this move will take some adjusting. "I hear you, buddy. Let's get you settled."

I need to find my bathroom, then I'll get them set up with a litter box, food, and water, and let them adjust to a smaller space before they venture farther.

I continue to the room at the end of the hallway with one cat carrier in each hand and can't stifle the sharp inhale when I enter.

What must be a king-sized bed with cream color fabric headboard sits centered on the far wall painted dark slate blue, bedside tables with stylish-looking lamps nestled atop each one. The bedding is various colors of cream and dove gray I wouldn't have imagined together, but they seem both clean and inviting. There's a blond wood dresser against the wall to my right with a mirror overtop, and the doors to what must be the closet and bathroom are on the opposite wall.

This man either has the best sense of style I've ever experienced in real life, or he hired a decorator who did their job like the bossiest of decorating bosses. Either way, I would be very comfortable here.

He's given me *his* room, I'm certain of it. No way is this a guest room. We'll be having words about this later, but for now, I drag my two giant suitcases inside and tuck them next to a long chest of drawers that—yep, he's emptied out for me.

I haven't pinned him down yet. He's been grumpy and withholding in every interaction we've had since we met last year... until he found me crying. Until he proposed marriage to help me—and yes, to help himself. But his reasons for doing this feel thin compared to what I'm getting out of it.

I've poked at him in our past interactions because that's my nature, but when it came time... when I needed help, *he* offered.

When I first got hurt, I thought I'd be able to recover. No insurance, sure, but I sunnily thought "I'll handle this."

Ah, sweet summer child.

When I lost the partner who'd committed to opening the café with me the same day I found out about the surgery, my dreams went up in smoke.

Or, less eloquently, they went up in miles and miles of medical bills.

It still burns through me when I think about it—on one hand understanding the delay changed their ability to invest, and on the other, feeling frustrated they couldn't give me more time.

I didn't tell Grace until after I'd decided to take Gruff up on his offer. It'd taken the knowledge that I had a way to solve the problem before I could bring myself to lay it on her —and she was furious with me for not telling her what was going on or asking her for help, especially since her career as a nurse would give her insights no one else in my life had. But with all the issues I've been having... the doctors are saying all these pesky problems like low energy, poor sleep, brittle nails and hair, and apparently even *bones* will be improved, if not solved completely, with surgery.

So. I had Gruff's offer, a contract signed, and I told Grace. I hadn't told her about the plan for the wedding... I hadn't wanted her to talk me out of it. I'd cracked a joke a while back about wishing I could find someone to marry and be my sugar daddy, and we'd laughed.

Cut to today when I married a man I barely know for his apartment and his insurance. A man in a very nice-looking uniform with a dark green jacket and tan pants with brown polished leather shoes and a hat he took off when he walked inside and later replaced when we exited City Hall. It made him look particularly dashing, him in his uniform with his widow's peak and his crow's feet at the corners of his gray-blue eyes and... whew.

Married.

And in return?

He needs something from me, and I confirmed it isn't physical. I mean honestly, ew, and also, there is no world in which this man couldn't find himself some physical atten-tion if he wanted it.

He'd said we'd go to his family's Christmas gathering to be seen together, and it was that simple—so here we are. And I am probably an idiot, although Grace's husband, JJ, who is an actual Army lawyer, reviewed the contract I signed weeks ago one last time *this morning* and promised me it's equitable.

So tonight, when he gets home, I'll try out having a man

as a roommate—er, *house*mate. Not just *a man*, but Wilson Gruff, perpetually frowning, extremely uptight, and too handsome and generous for his or my own good.

Should be fun.

CHAPTER NINE

Gruff

Entering my own home and finding all the lights on at eight o'clock at night is less dreadful than I thought it would be.

Admittedly, I've spent the afternoon doing my level best not to think about Andy coming to live with me. I specifically avoided being at the house so she could adjust without me hovering over her, and yet, I've mentally hovered. Did she do too much, even though the movers should've done all the heavy lifting? Will she be comfortable?

It's not like we're actually married, nor are we friends. This is both better for my expectations and worse, because I don't know her well enough to have any expectations.

At the same time, we *are* actually married. But not. Because there's no love involved here. This helps.

But she is another person in my space, so that tells me enough about why I'm dreading the larger set-up here. I've lived alone since my divorce five years ago. In this time, I've embraced that I'm the kind of man who is meant to be alone.

JJ once accused me of being a misanthrope. I told him to shove it.

I don't hate people, but I hate the imposition of catering to someone's needs when I don't know what they are. So that's why, even though Andy and I have signed a contract agreeing to the basic tenets of our marriage—duration up to six months, financial separation, obligations, basic responsibilities in terms of rent (none, since I own the home and she's not giving me a dime), etc., I can't be sure how this'll go.

My ill-timed TDY this past month kept me away from both her and my mother. In each case, there's positive and negative aspects to the distance. The downside to missing a few more in-person interactions with Andy is that now I'm on my own to figure things out with her post-marriage.

It's weird.

I shut the front door softly, just in case she's in bed—does she go to bed this early? I think she still works at Alex Brews, so she's probably early to bed, but again, it's one more thing I'm clueless about.

Something brushes against my leg, and even though logically I know it's not a snake slithering up my pant leg on a cold late-November evening, I am not entirely logical.

Nor is the sound that emerges from my mouth—a yelp-squeal kind of noise I'm certain I've never made before right as I step on something long and squiggly—wait, is it actually a snake?—and then the most unearthly sound from the depths of the earth hits my ears. It's a yowl and a rumble and definitely not a snake-like sound, so there's a small mercy.

I stumble, tripping over whatever brushed my leg, and scamper down the hallway into the well-lit kitchen right as Andy slides across the polished wood flooring with wide eyes and a large book in her hand raised like a weapon.

"What—"

"Gah!" she says, throwing the book at me before she can stop herself.

I shield myself with my hands, bracing for impact, but it doesn't come. The book flies past me, thunking against the wall. It lands with a loud *thwap* and there's a beat of silence.

"I'm so sorry. I am so, so sorry." Andy rushes me, pulling on my arm to get a look at me. Her bright blue eyes are slipping over every inch of me, searching for injuries despite her book failing to make contact.

Her hand on my arm is determined, but gentle. And it's the oddest response I could possibly have, considering the upheaval to my life evidenced so clearly by the last fifteen seconds, but my heart does... something. Not galloping after a feral beast attack or stuttering as she tossed a book, but... something else.

Not sure what. But it does something it hasn't for as long as I can remember.

Exhales, maybe.

"I'm fine. You didn't even hit me," I say, grasping her wrist and removing her hand from my arm.

The contact seems to jar her into reality, and she gapes at me, then chuckles. "You're right. I'm... I'm so sorry." She looks to be holding back tears, but then she covers her mouth, and a larger laugh sneaks out. "I'm so, so sorry I threw a book at you. Ol' lefty's aim isn't awesome, but for once, that's probably for the best."

She waves her left hand and I realize she must be

avoiding using the right, the one she broke which has a brace on it, whenever possible.

She adds, "Not a great way to welcome home my new husband on our wedding night, is it?"

And this statement, these words, are what tip me over, pouring out the stress and frustration from the day. This woman whom I barely know, who just attempted to defend herself from an intruder with a large paperback book, she's my wife.

Her cat, the beast I must've stepped on when I entered, is pacing, a miniature orange and white striped lion, like I've offended it with my presence in my own home. Andy's just literally thrown a book at me, and I have no idea what I'm doing, but I start laughing.

"Lovely greeting," I say, then another rumble of laughter trips out.

Andy's gaze shoots up to me and her smile broadens, almost impossibly wide. She's laughing hard enough now she can't speak, and a tear leaks from the corner of her eye as she scrunches them both shut.

And goodness, she's beautiful. I've known it well enough since the first time I saw her and seeing her in her wedding dress earlier confirmed it. Only an idiot wouldn't admit to it. But right here, in her sweatpants and make up-free face, her laughter coming free and open, she is...

I swallow hard, clearing my throat against whatever thought was about to materialize, and straighten. *Bad idea.*

"I'll just get changed and we can get this done." I brush past her and yes, it's abrupt and I'm sure she's trying to figure out what just happened to make me suck every bit of humor and fun out of the moment, but oh well. A glance at my pants legs shows a swath of white and pale orange fur all the way from the hem to mid-calf. The cat did this. Looks like I'll need to invest in a heavy-duty lint roller to clean up my uniform now.

I can't be sharing little moments like this with her. It's not what we're doing here and it's not why she's here. Best to stay focused on the reasons we agreed to this arrangement... and figure out how I make sure her cat doesn't attack me every time I walk in the door.

CHAPTER TEN

Andy

Laughing with Gruff was unexpected.

It only happened one other time and it was a far shorter moment than this. It was months ago, the night of Grace and JJ's second wedding, and, well, I don't feel like harkening back to it because right now I'm trying to figure out how to move forward past the twisty jab of disappointment blooming in my chest.

Why would I be disappointed by Colonel Wilson Gruff showing me his sense of humor is exactly as I thought it was —a fleeting and false little wisp of a thing? He probably just met his laughter quota for the holiday season.

Farewell, lovely smile. See you again sometime next spring.

I scoop up PB and cradle him like the baby he is. "You can't be in his face yet. I don't think he realized you'd be roaming free."

Honestly, I didn't think he'd be out this soon, either. I touch my forehead to his furry orange and white one, and his little purr box ignites, sending feline vibrations rumbling through his chest cavity.

Setting him down gently, I work to calm myself. I'm still on a little adrenaline high from the fear of an intruder and then the laugh attack. And, sure, there's the small thrill of seeing Gruff enter the house like he owns the place and belongs here, because he does. He's all tall and serious with the uniform he wore at our ceremony giving him the cut of a professional and a soldier at the same time. He's so masculine it's foreign to me since my main interactions with the male population lately have been with my darling neutered boy cats.

It's weird that this—his uniform and his sharp jaw and his rightful sense of ownership over his own house—is a thing I enjoy, and yet I do.

Trick is, I don't belong here. And I'm not sure how long it'll take me to feel I do. Maybe I won't ever, and that's okay. I'm only going to be here for six months *max*, so it's worth embracing that I may not ever feel like this is home.

In truth, I haven't felt at home in a while. It's less to do with the place and more to do with feeling settled in myself. Ever since my rolling ball of medical debt stole my plans and dream, I can't seem to get my footing.

"Ready?" Gruff asks, his voice traveling from his room down the hall—which yes, I have avoided snooping around during my six hours alone in the place—as I'm pulling out one of the low barstools situated at the kitchen island.

He pulls one out, too, and I see he's not wearing the same clothes. I expected to have a little sweatpants party here in the kitchen, but the man has put on stiff-looking dark jeans and a long-sleeved shirt that appears very soft.

It's the first time I've seen him in something other than a button-up shirt and suit jacket or Army uniform. It showcases the now very apparent reality that Gruff is a man with a steely gaze and a steelier body.

The pecs and the way the soft material molds over the firm curves of his shoulders and chest... *chef's kiss.*

"Is this for me?" He gestures to the mug of peppermint tea on the counter.

I jerk my eyes away from his too-appealing shirt—it's the shirt, obviously, and not the man wearing it because I'm simply not the kind of woman who drools over muscles—and nod like a maniac.

"Yes. Thought it might be nice. It's cold out there." Hopefully, he can follow that train of thought.

"It is." He swipes at his phone and sets it down. "So you have a cat."

I swallow the steaming hot liquid of my mug with a gulp that sends burning tea down my throat and partially into my windpipe—perfect!

It's awkward as I sputter and cough behind my elbow, but finally confirm. "Yes. Well, two, actually, but the other one is an anti-social misanthrope so you're unlikely to see him anytime soon."

His gaze narrows. "Two cats."

I know not everyone loves cats. Of course I do. It may or may not play into why I didn't mention them, though in truth we didn't specifically cover pets, and in the flurry of the last few weeks of getting this arranged and my apartment packed up, I failed to mention it.

"Yeah. Sorry. Is that a dealbreaker?"

His blue eyes pin me for a few seconds longer than is comfortable. "Bit late now."

I chuckle like, "Haha! Good one!" but I don't say that

because we both know it's not a joke. It's his acceptance of his fate to be roommates with two cats and their crazy cat lady mom, and he's got no way of getting out of it unless he wants to annul the deal, but he's also got motivation to keep this together, at least for a little while, so again, here we are.

"So the one you met is PB and the other one is shy. You won't really see him but he's all black and his name is RJ."

His eyes narrow and I expect him to ask what the initials stand for like most people do, but he simply blinks.

I do the same because this is going just swimmingly.

"Have you scheduled your surgery?" he asks, scrolling down what I think is a list on his phone.

"Uh, no. I think you have to enroll me in your insurance, and then I can start working on referrals and stuff. I don't think it'll happen before the end of the year at this point since most surgical schedules are already pretty full through the holidays."

I've talked this through with Grace and she has enough connections in the medical world, she confirmed it'd be unlikely. Plus, I'm joining a whole new healthcare system, and they aren't likely to let me skip over all the initial appointments and just outright schedule surgery.

"Of course. I'll get that done as soon as possible. We'll need to get you your military ID as soon as we can. I'll check for appointments. That's first, I think." His brow furrows. "And honestly, I'm not certain what else. I'll figure it out."

"Thanks," I say, because that is the whole point, at least from my side of things.

I wait for him to bring up *his* end of this bargain, but he doesn't. Because I'm just that kind of person, I nudge. "So, um... what about your part of the deal? When do we do that?"

He shifts on the stool and our knees brush. All of a sudden, he strikes me as a rather large human. I know he's tall—of course he is. I'm just... feeling it now. Have his shoulders always been this broad? Is he actually *that* much taller than me?

"It will primarily center around the holidays."

I blink, anticipating more... nothing. "So like, Christmas Eve? Day? New Year's? More?"

He nods.

"At your parents' house? Where do they live?" Because so far I have no information, so I need everything to fill in the gaps. He's only said he wants to reassure his parents that he's doing well.

His father is a retired senator who I'm pretty sure lives here since Grace and JJ have been to their fancy mansion, if I'm correctly remembering what Grace reported last year.

"We'll go back and forth to my parents' home in the DC. May need to spend the night on Christmas Eve—it's a bit of a tradition. The room I typically stay in has a couch and a bed, so that's no issue. If it's not going well, we can easily sneak out before bed and go back for Christmas morning." His eyes find mine. "I apologize I didn't mention the plan sooner."

Okay. Sleepover at the in-laws! Should be awkward, but fine. We'll handle it, and it's one night. I can't tell if there's more going on than wanting his family to see that he's settled and stable, but I can't pin it down, and maybe it's just the growing pains of figuring out how to communicate.

"I'll have to ask for the time off, but it should be fine. We're closed Christmas day, at least." And I'll need to make my excuses with my folks, but they wouldn't have expected me for more than an overnight anyway. Not that he seems prone to asking personal questions, but I don't want to deal with the whole parent thing tonight, so I don't mention it. They are such a small part of my life and I've accepted that, so keeping all of these things from them is simple. They don't need to know about any of this because it'll all be over in a matter of months.

"I appreciate it." He taps his phone again. "I have an early morning, so if there's nothing else?"

His brows raise like he expects me to protest, or maybe like I'm his secretary and I've inconvenienced him. I can't read him well at all, so I just wave him away. Guess I'll have a bowl of cereal for dinner—I kind of thought we'd eat together tonight so I waited, but that's fine. I want to ask if he's eaten, but it feels like an invasion of his privacy or something. Definitely going to take a minute to get used to how all this will work.

"Nope. All good here."

And it is. It's fine that I'm going to bed in a stranger's house with the sudden ability to file my taxes jointly with someone. Not that we will—we worked out the financial aspects of this arrangement before we did anything else.

I'm getting what I want and need out of this deal, so I'll just ignore the niggling feeling I've done something today that'll change... not just my situation temporarily, but everything.

Gruff

A week into my marriage, the headache starts at my temples and works its way behind my eyes. By the time my mother calls me on my drive home from work, I can hardly listen to her speak without wincing.

"Don't be angry with your brother."

I do not respond.

"This year will be different because you've got your Andy, right?" she prods, though her voice holds a pleasure I can hear despite the noise clutter of the cars around me.

I exhale, flicking my blinker as I join the long line of people turning left across traffic. How is there traffic at seven p.m. on a Friday night? That's just the glorious reality of working and living in the Washington, DC area. There is always traffic, especially if you're on the way home from work.

"I do have Andy," I say, my heart so far from in it.

"I know you two got together quickly, but it's a wise decision. Marrying a woman who cares for you will make your life better."

I open my mouth wide, stretching my jaw muscles and rolling back my shoulders, begging my body to hold out a while longer before it completely shuts down with a full-blown migraine.

"Yes, Mother."

What else can I say? She knows it was quick with me and Andy, but she doesn't realize *how* quick. She was made to believe we'd been interested in each other since we met a year ago, that we'd dated since JJ's wedding in the summer, and that we'd done the courthouse thing because neither of us wanted a big wedding. I don't think she realizes Andy is the friend I mentioned at tea, the one she challenged me to help at any cost.

She claims she understands.

But my mother is one of the smartest people I know. I love her more than I love pretty much anyone else, so I can acknowledge this and yet admit her tendency to push when she wants something. She pushed me toward Andy with a few well-placed comments and now here I am. Again, she may not know she did this, but the reality is, I was already on my way to helping Andy, but my mother's speech about all the privileges I had struck home and I did what I could, unconventional though it is.

Plus, the fact that she hasn't arrived at my doorstep demanding to meet her new daughter-in-law suggests she has an unexpected amount of patience regarding our relationship, and this alone is enough to make me suspect *she* suspects something.

"Don't say it like that. I know it's new, but you know how to work hard, don't you?"

I turn onto my street, relief already flooding in at the familiar trees lining the quaint section of Old Town Alexandria.

"It's not about that." She can't really believe I've already moved past the change in plans. "I'm going to have to redo leave forms, and I have to ask Andy to do the same. It's..." Ultimately, I don't care all that much about the change in schedule for those reasons. What I do have a problem with is... everything else.

"Again, don't be angry with—"

"It's not anger, Mother. It's simply acknowledging the change in plans, and the reality that it creates a bit of a headache for me." And it is so typical of Jason to expect everyone to collapse into his plan, his schedule, his needs.

"Do you have some Tylenol? You should take something. Maybe lie down."

I pull into my spot, relieved to see my front door. "I'll be fine. Thanks for checking in."

She can hear I'm done and doesn't belabor the conversation. I shouldn't be so short with her, nor should I blame her for the way the world collapses around my youngest brother's life in a way that often leaves me scrambling to catch my breath and force away a rising resentment I'm not proud of.

And now, if Andy's home, I'll have to go in and tell her the short visit to DC we'd planned on for Christmas is now a *five*-day trek to Vermont.

I've hardly seen my new wife, but she's left little signs of life, and then there are her cats. I've only seen the one, who favors curling up on the back of the couch in the living room and leaving his cat hair all over my clothing, but I'm loosely aware of the other's existence.

"I'm so glad you're home," Andy says, greeting me from the kitchen where she's wearing...

I clear my throat. "Oh?" I ask, because finding actual words isn't going to happen. She's wearing an apron.

Don't come for me. I can't verbalize why, but something about an apron just kind of kills me, and the way the strings lace around her waist makes me want to set my hands there...

"I made us a celebratory dinner because I was able to make my appointment with the specialist today for the week before Christmas and I'm just..." She swipes a finger under her eye. "I'm so grateful to you. Thank you."

Horror slips through me and my brain pulses angrily like a bulb turning on too bright before flickering out. I've seen her cry before, but she didn't start while I watched, helpless like an imbecile to do anything to comfort her. Last time, I was too worried about her, too focused on solving the problem.

My mother never cries. She's the embodiment of her British ancestry and her politician's wife ilk with her stiff upper lip and steely determination. My ex didn't cry either —she was generally emotionally inaccessible, but then again, so was I.

"I'm glad."

Stilted and awkward as it comes out, she just beams at me.

And then, as though she's done it a hundred times before, she launches herself into my arms.

With zero time to brace for impact, her arms wrap around me right as I let out a low grunt when she hits me with the force of her cheer and excitement. She is a sunshine wrecking ball in a Christmas tree apron and has no idea.

My brain rattles inside my skull and I cringe against the pain. Her arms squeeze, then release, and she backs away, still smiling, until she sees my face.

"Did I hurt you?"

She grabs my wrist and her blue eyes peer up into mine with so much concern, just looking at her almost makes me feel better.

What an odd thought.

"No, no. I have a migraine coming on. I just need to head to bed."

Her face falls and she looks truly devastated, like hearing I'm in pain makes her hurt.

"I'm so sorry. Let me get you some water. Should you eat something?" She bustles into the kitchen, quickly filling a tall glass with cool water from the dispenser in the freezer door and shoving it into one of my empty hands.

"Thank you," I say, taking the glass and finding I have no idea what to do with myself now. I want to be horizontal in a dark room in a silent house, but I can't do that now, can I? "I don't know if I can eat."

She studies me from closer than before, then reaches up and gently slides her fingers over the short hair brushing my forehead. It's gotten too long. I'm overdue for a cut.

That feels so good.

"You poor thing. Go to bed. Text me if you need anything. You won't know I'm here." And then, she picks up my bag and literally ushers me down the hallway to the door of my room.

I've hardly spoken, and I still have no cogent thought to share. I can't remember what I'm supposed to talk to her about, something nagging from before I got home, so I just... go inside. I strip down to my boxer briefs and slug back some high-powered pain reliever my doctor gave me for times like these and slide into my bed with a prayer for relief and maybe not too terrible of a time this go round.

I fall asleep thinking about cool fingers on my forehead and crystalline blue eyes and apron strings.

CHAPTER TWELVE

Andy

Two.

The number of miles I've paced around the living room in the last hour.

My worry is most likely misplaced, but... what if it's not? I've gone from, "he just needs some rest" to "what if it's so bad he's incapacitated on the floor and can't speak because he's in so much pain and he's waiting for you to come save him," to "he's probably in a coma." I don't have a ton of experience with migraines, and searching the internet has both calmed and lit my fear on fire with some kerosene for pizzazz.

Seeing a man like Gruff look so miserable has disarmed me in a way I haven't experienced since my only medical malady parade started nine months ago. It gives me a sense of doom and I hate it.

I'd been overflowing with gratitude, feeling so light and

hopeful that this unusual set-up we've chosen is really going to work now that I've got my doctor's appointment scheduled.

I want to check on him, but I can't. He shut his door. We aren't friends.

Spouses? Sure. Friends?

Nah. Not yet.

But also, I'll be held liable if he's in there dying and I just, what? Stay out here for the sake of propriety or something?

"We can't leave him to die, right?" I ask PB.

His orange tail switches.

"I take that as an agreement. Thing is... I can't be the one to open the door. So... could you?" In my dreams, this is when my feline genius would hear me, understand me, and do my bidding.

Alas, the key word in the previous sentence is *feline*, and therefore, there will be no obeisance. This is one of many reasons I love cats.

"But I could go for a more cooperative one."

I pace another circle around the gorgeous living room, eying the corner I've imagined a Christmas tree in a few times since Thanksgiving came and went last week. I don't love the holiday, and apparently since Gruff's family celebrates Christmas together, they do their own thing for Thanksgiving. I mostly stayed out of his way when it became clear he had no plans to make plans and was ultimately gone most of the day itself. Fine by me. Grace and Justin were visiting family, so the cats and I just had a relaxing day at home watching movies and drawing.

PB skitters down the hallway and I take his lead, inching close to Gruff's door and leaning an ear against it.

Total silence.

I exhale a heavy breath and shrug at my cat, who blinks slowly, then turns his butt and saunters away like he thinks I'll enjoy the view.

"What a butthead!" I hiss at him, because how dare he leave me here to ponder my human responsibilities?

Grace's response to my earlier concerned deluge of texts assured me he's probably fine. She and JJ haven't heard anything about Gruff having chronic migraines, so maybe this is a one-off.

Maybe my being here is part of the cause? Maybe he's deeply allergic to the cats and the primary symptom is brain-splitting headaches?

I distract myself for another hour before I finally let myself into his room as quietly as I can.

Then I gasp so loud the neighboring townhouse must hear me. Fortunately, Gruff sleeps through my not-so-subtle response to his room.

Because this is not a real room. It's a library or office and it is, even in the darkness lit only by the light coming from the hallway, gorgeous.

Ceiling-high shelves lined with books everywhere, light touches in a dark wood I can't quite see the color of, and a couch that evidently folds out into a bed. It's half as big as the primary bedroom he gave me, and it... it just doesn't make sense. Why not put me in here? Why would he surrender his gorgeous, huge bed and ensuite bathroom in order to sleep in here?

Weirdo. And maybe one more thing contributing to his migraines if his pull-out bed is on par with any I've ever slept on. *Mm, yes, this metal bar does feel great jabbing directly into my spine, thank you for designing it thus.*

I watch, waiting to see his chest rise and fall. He's

curled on his side so I can't see his face, and an instinct to stroke his hair and whisper reassurances grips me.

I resist because I am not insane, and I know that's crossing a line.

Letting him sleep is the best thing I can do for him now, Grace confirmed after my concerned texts earlier. Hopefully, he took some medicine and it'll all be fine.

When I finally go to bed, I dream about a moment at Grace's wedding last summer. I'm standing at the side of a wood-planked dance floor with twinkly lights overhead, swaying to the music with my third glass of champagne in hand like it's my date.

Gruff appears like a grumbling shadow next to me, and I don't have to look to know he's brought his storm cloud energy to bear on the gravity around me. Everything gets heavier, tilting slightly toward the black hole of him.

"Enjoying the party?" I ask, because I can't resist. He won't ignore me if I talk to him, though if I don't start, he's unlikely to utter a word.

He hums, a more congenial sound than I've heard from him in... ever. This has me glancing up at him—and it is up, because I've already abandoned the strappy sandals I wore for the ceremony, and he is six-something, plus his grumbly energy gives him an extra inch or two.

"I agree. It is lovely. I'm so happy for them." I say this with a wide smile I genuinely feel. I am thrilled for Grace and JJ—delighted I've gotten to see their relationship go from deal-making marriage to desperately in love, and now embracing the reality that despite their beginnings, they're made for each other.

It's so freaking romantic. And I'm not even particularly a romantic at heart. I just love love, and I love that my friend has found it with a good man.

"I fail to see how it'll last, but it's good they can enjoy it while it does, I suppose."

I shoot him a glare because who says that at someone's wedding? "Seriously? Why would they not last?"

He gives me a look like I'm the idiot for not already knowing how their marriage will end—as though it's a foregone conclusion it will.

"Half of marriages end in divorce. It's inevitable."

I roll my eyes. "Well, that's the difference between us. You see half as *inevitable,* and I see half as hopeful. As a world of possibilities."

He scoffs, though it's not loud and obnoxious. More genuinely surprised someone could think this way. "Well, how unfortunate for you. I imagine you live with disappointment all day, every day."

My mouth drops open, but for once in my life, I don't have a response. I'll blame the champagne. So, weirdly, I reach up and shove his shoulder. "Rude."

His brows raise. "Did you just... push me?"

I tuck my lips between my teeth as the reality that yes, I did just push this man hits me with cruel clarity. "Um. Yeah. Sorry. Let's call it a hopeful push. That's a thing, right? You've experienced that?"

His brows drop low now. He is not impressed. *Cool.*

"I'm sorry. That was inappropriate, even if you are deeply unpleasant." I chuckle, then gasp. "Okay, I'm sorry about that, too."

I wouldn't be shocked if he huffed and marched away to

a dark corner, but instead, his eyes narrow. And something in my belly swoops when his gaze catches mine and he says, "You have a mouth on you, don't you?"

Heat flows like lava from my belly and out to every limb, burning in my cheeks and causing my chest and neck to flush.

"I—"

Again, he's made me speechless.

And those eyes... his lashes are long and dark—of course. Because he definitely doesn't appreciate them. But here I am, marveling. Practically lapping up the attention he's giving me, and willing him to... something.

Do something.

A flash of fantasy crosses my mind—he could lean in. He could say something else. He could set a hand over the satin at my waist and whisper in my ear.

But he does none of that.

He only stares a moment longer—one heartbeat, two— then steps away with a muttered "excuse me" and disappears into the crowd of onlookers.

I turn back and watch JJ and Grace finish up their dance, a handful of couples swirling around with them. I set my hand on my neck and exhale with a laugh. Did I really just get all wound up over that man?

We've only argued when we talk. We send little jabs one another's way and don't seem to agree on anything.

So what on Earth was that?

When I wake hours later, the memory of the dreamy interaction at the wedding fresh on my mind and remarkably like what happened in real life, I've lost the objectivity I somehow managed the last few weeks.

I've steadily ignored the reality that I find Wilson Gruff extremely attractive because his personality is in equal measure unattractive.

But now he's more human to me. I've seen snatches of who he is and it's not all bad. Of course, I wouldn't bind myself legally to someone I think is actually morally reprehensible or anything, but now I know things I can't unknow.

He's super good at decorating a house. He's got great taste. He apparently likes books enough to have an entire library in his small home. He's kind of a mama's boy, but there's tough stuff in his family dynamic that drove him to marry me, and I feel in my gut I'm going to find out and it's not going to make this any better.

But who am I kidding? This is a man who I *used to* find unpleasant, but now I know. He's secretly a supremely decent person. He may not've gifted me said library and is instead holed up there pretending it's an actual second bedroom instead of a fancy office with built-in bookshelves and a pull-out couch, but he's giving some serious Beauty and the Beast vibes.

He's secretly kind of a hero.

I'm getting the better end of this bargain by far. Unless his family is a pack of wild wolves that he's going to feed me to in a matter of weeks, I'm coming out ahead here. From what I know, he's more likely to save me from wolves than feed me to them, though.

It may have been his idea, but I won't let this arrangement be something I feel guilty about, and this right here is a perfect moment for me to help him. I can take care of him —as my instinct tells me to do. Right?

Or does he need to be left alone? Normally he wouldn't have company, and I've already spiraled through all the ways my being here with the boys might be causing him *more* pain. But no, I don't want to make excuses and stay away if I can do anything to help. Get him water? Food? More medicine? Ice pack or heating pad or whatever someone needs when they have a migraine?

All of this muddled thinking is why I pad down the hallway at six in the morning and enter his room without knocking.

CHAPTER THIRTEEN

Gruff

When Andy slips into my room, I'm still groggy and half-waking. I'm sitting on the edge of my bed, elbows on knees, hands in my hair, thumbs lightly massaging my temples, willing away the nausea.

Her intake of breath when she realizes I'm awake draws my eye.

"I'm sorry. I just got worried. I'm not great at ignoring the 'uh oh' feeling so I decided to just come check on you. How are you?" She twists her fingers together in front of her, maybe in an effort to obscure the fact that she's wearing only a pair of tiny shorts and a tank top.

"I'll live," I say, voice like I've swallowed gravel. I still feel like squinting away from the light, but the harshest pain in my head has subsided.

"Good. Can I get you anything? Coffee? Food?"

I look away from her wide eyes and the miles of skin left

bare right now, mostly because I want to keep looking so very much. And we can't have that.

"I should probably eat. You don't have to do anything." Why is everything I say so wrong? I don't know how to thank her for her concern but get her to leave. She shouldn't be in here. I can't have her in this space, too.

"I don't mind. Really. I can run out and grab something or scramble some eggs."

She's waiting for a response from me, and I just don't have any to give. Since I can't find the words, I push off the bed and stand, rolling my neck and praying the migraine will stay gone. My stomach lurches and I wish I'd been able to eat last night.

"I—"

I glance up when her voice cuts off. Her gaze is sliding over my chest and down my stomach. She's registering I'm wearing only my boxer briefs and she's seeing just about all of me. Even with the groggy hangover-like fog muffling my mind, a swoop of pleasure glides through me at the way her cheeks are tinged pink.

She bites her bottom lip.

I clear my throat.

She whirls around instantly. "Um, so yeah. I'll go get the coffee started and just... yeah."

She scoots out the door and leaves me standing, barely a whole human, and yet heart pumping with more will and energy than I've had in recent memory.

Half an hour later, I've showered and dressed myself with as much speed as I can muster while also babying my brain and attempting to keep my limbs loose. The tendency to hunch or shrink up is ever present, but letting muscles bunch into tight knots will not help the situation.

"There's eggs with a little cheese and toast here, if you can stomach it. And coffee. And water. Is there anything else I can get for you?" She's flittering around the kitchen like a hummingbird, more anxious than I've ever seen her.

How did this woman seem so relaxed and perfectly calm at our wedding and yet she's visibly stressed right now? She's probably aggravating that wrist she should be resting. Instead, she's worried about me.

Maybe seeing me half-naked made her uncomfortable and she doesn't realize it was a mistake? I didn't mean for her to see me like that.

My heart sinks with a new thought. Maybe, despite all behavior to the contrary, she's like my ex was. She's that particular kind of fragile manufactured to react to any possible trigger and rooted in, primarily, wanting what she wants when she wants it. And I've broken something already.

"I'm sorry if I've made you uncomfortable. I didn't mean to be inappropriate. I honestly forgot I hadn't put on pajamas." My cheeks heat in a way that feels positively foreign to me.

Her head snaps up. "You don't have to apologize. I came into your room and invaded your privacy. *I'm* the one who should be sorry."

"I appreciate that, but no. This is on me." Something sour swirls in my gut and I'm clenching my teeth with regret, then instantly wishing I hadn't because my whole head is still tender.

Her gaze narrows. "What is *this*? Like, where did the apology come from?" She wipes a rag over the counter in front of her.

I reach for the glass of water and take a seat on the same barstool I used last night. "I've upset you. That deserves an apology."

Her eyes narrow into slits as she stands there, studying me, then inches closer so she's no longer on the opposite side of the kitchen island.

"I think..." She frowns down at the countertop. "I think maybe we've gotten our wires crossed."

Everything in me has seized up, a familiar dread wringing my neck as my shaking hand rises to my heart. I stand, ready to give her space, but my legs go weak, and I land back on the stool with a brain-juddering knock. "I'm sorry. I don't—"

Her hands are on me in seconds, the left at my shoulder, the right covering the one over my heart. "Please stop apologizing. Everything is fine."

Big blue eyes blink back at me, waiting. I study her, heart thundering under my palm, and wait. Rather than back away or lose her patience, she slides her hand to my neck and rolls her fingers into the tense muscles there even as she laces her right hand with my left, still pressed over my heart.

"Everything is fine. Can you say it?" Her voice is endlessly gentle and confident.

Finally, it clicks.

I come back to the moment *here* and *now* and not some version of my past with someone who isn't Andy. This woman isn't shrinking or hiding or wishing she could escape and coating every interaction with resentment. I don't know exactly why she was buzzing around the kitchen, but did I really confuse it with my ex's way of showing me she wasn't happy?

She had been excellent at letting me know how she felt, but she'd hardly ever deigned to do so with words.

And here's Andy, gaze pinning me in place and words clear and everything so straightforward, I'm not sure I can handle this any better than I can what I thought was happening seconds ago.

But I do as she says. "Everything is fine."

Her lips curve into a soft smile. "Good."

We stay like this, connected for another moment, and then she steps away, removing her lovely, warm hands and taking her minty-sweety scent, that I am deeply sad to be deprived of, with her.

"I'm sorry," I say again, because I am compelled to try to explain.

She whirls around and gives me a half-lidden glare. "Wilson Gruff, you have to stop apologizing."

I huff out a breath that turns into a laugh because she's so peeved by me and again, it hits me how unlike anyone I've ever known she is. And, frankly, how much I like this about her.

She's not sullen and punishing. She's tossing me fake scowls because that's what they are—fake. She's too damn sunny and wants to lighten every moment, like she's doing right now, and even acknowledging this sends a wave of relief through me again. She's joking, not letting me take all the blame for a simple misunderstanding. She's talking to me without saying one thing and meaning something entirely different.

"I will apologize if I want. I accept that you were in my room, and I don't need to apologize for that, but I will say

I'm sorry for just now. My previous marriage had some challenging dynamics and I just need to remember..."

I search for the right way to put it, but she asks, "What? Remember what?"

With her lovely filled-with-expectation tone and her expression earnest, I can't help but tell her the truth. "That you are the complete opposite of my ex-wife."

CHAPTER FOURTEEN

Andy

Not long after we had what I'm calling our *moment,* those delicious few seconds when we cleared the air of misunderstanding and our eyes were still locked and my hand was on his ridiculously appealing chest, I tuck myself away in my room to clean up for the day and, in all honesty, hide away and ponder his statement.

On one hand, I'm inclined to believe that being different from a man's *ex* is a good thing, or at least could be a good thing if he ultimately didn't click with her. But on the other hand, the awkward one where I don't admit I care, he married his first wife, presumably, for love. So like, he probably found her attractive and liked her personality.

This gives me a fleeting sense of being marital chopped liver. Maybe not actual chopped liver, but like... having an *eau de liver* or something.

Also, I have no idea why I'm thinking about chopped

liver nor do I actually know what chopped liver smells or tastes or even looks like, but I did just recently buy PB and RJ new treats that are, of course, liver flavor.

And I think that's all the time in my life I'm going to give to this inane line of thought.

After that lovely little poor me spiral, I snuggle each of my mangey little cats, then slip into the shower. An hour after I left him, PB leads me into the living room where I find Gruff relaxed into his soft couch... watching a movie.

"What the heck? Where did that TV come from?"

He looks puzzled. "It's always there."

I look more closely and realize, sure enough, the artwork I thought adorned the area over his mantel is, in fact, a TV. "That is so fancy."

He gives me a half-smile that makes me feel twisty inside.

"I didn't realize, but... thank you? Does this mean you've been sitting in here and not using the TV? I'm sorry I didn't ever give you a tour of the house."

I wave him away. "Not an issue. I don't do a ton of TV regularly, and I've been plowing through Christmas romances, so I've had plenty to entertain me."

PB jumps up and finds his spot on the back of the couch. I keep my attention on Gruff to gauge how he feels about the new feline perch. He doesn't seem bothered, but this man has a history of hiding feelings, I am certain.

"Are you going out?"

I turn to find his gaze in the general vicinity of my legs and likely the bright red tights I'm wearing under my cute sparkly miniskirt before they slide to my face. If I didn't know for certain the skirt isn't *too* mini, I might worry I'm revealing too much based on the rather intense way he was looking.

"Yes. Grace and I are having lunch. I've gone too long without Mexican food, so she's going to solve this crisis by feeding me guacamole." I grin because just the thought of the meal to come makes me want to smile.

He frowns, not hiding a very clear broadcast of disappointment.

"Should I... not? Did you need me for something?" I cross to the couch but I'm reaching for my phone, pulling up my text thread with Grace.

"No. Nothing like that. I do need to talk to you about a few things. Just a few minutes when you have time." He steals his gaze from mine and centers it forward, like he assumes I'll be leaving now.

Silly man.

I round the couch and take a seat one cushion down from him. "Shoot, partner."

Instant regret.

Why am I a cartoon version of myself around him sometimes? I'm either pinging around the kitchen nervously or I'm slinging out weird sayings like I'm in a spaghetti western... why?

Though to be fair, the me I am with myself is different these days, too. I'm a worn-down version of myself, a bit of used-up sandpaper that used to scratch off his paint and now barely makes a dent. It's not that I want to be butting heads with the man, nor would I now that I'm aware of who he actually is and not just who he comes off as socially, but it's another side effect of the last nine months taking their toll.

I guess weird western speak is not so terrible.

He sits up completely, taking his feet down from where they've been resting on the coffee table in front of him. "About Christmas."

"Okay. The plans with your family?"

"Yes."

He doesn't speak and my pulse jumps. "Is everything okay?"

He exhales and turns so his knees are pointed toward me, a deeply serious look on his handsome face.

"It is okay. But the plan has changed." His lips press together into a grim line, but thankfully, he continues before the suspense actually kills me. "The family will be doing Christmas at a ski lodge in Vermont."

I blink. "Vermont."

"From the twenty-first to the twenty-sixth."

I exhale. "For five nights."

He nods. "I think I can trim it down to four, maybe three."

Nothingness is all I hear for a few seconds as though this is an atomic bomb and not a slight change in plans. Sure, we're now spending five nights out of state rather than one night in the city next door to us, but this is not a crisis. It does feel significant, though, and I'm not sure it's because of *me*. It's his whole demeanor that's telling me we've got a huge challenge ahead.

"Okay. Okay.... Yeah. Totally fine. We can do that. Right?" I hope I can get off work—I planned to work as much as possible around the holidays. But that's fine. I wait for him to cheerily confirm we can totally do this. "Right?"

"Yes. Of course. It'll be fine. And there's plenty to do at the lodge, we can keep busy and ideally interact as little as possible with the family." Determination etches lines in his cheeks and slight wrinkles at the edges of his eyes.

For some dumb reason, he looks brutally attractive right now.

Not helpful, brain!

"Okay, cool. Then we'll probably need to talk through that a little more. Do you mind if I still head out to meet Grace? I can stay if you'd rather—"

"No, please. Go see Grace. Enjoy your guacamole."

"Happy to bring you some," I say, inflection making it a question.

A smile flits over his face, and he shakes his head just once. "No, thank you. Have fun."

I give him a smile because he's successfully shifted my mind back to something I can happily think about. "Thanks. Enjoy your show."

With a weird wave I lightly regret, I slip out the door, nudging PB back before I shut it, and then I begin my walk to Tacos y Tacos. Anticipation is positively rushing through my veins and I know it's not only for the guac or my friend time.

It's because of Gruff. *Will.* Maybe at some point, I'll get up the guts to call him that and see how it goes.

But for now, I'll let this fizzy, joyful feeling take over and banish the worry and the sense that maybe I'm missing something, and he has good reason to be scowling about this change.

For now, I'll savor the wreaths adorning every door and the garland wrapped around lampposts and the Christmas displays in the bookstore and flower shop windows, and I'll go eat some guacamole.

CHAPTER FIFTEEN

Gruff

I'm not sure how long Andy will be gone, but it's the first time in a while I didn't find an excuse to leave the house and stay out of her way.

The migraine left me absolutely exhausted though it was mercifully short. I've had one that lasted for four days and I've never been so miserable—truly, whether in a tent in the Afghan wilderness or rainy season in Iraq or the blazing summer heat of Kuwait, no physical discomfort is worse than the misery of a migraine.

Fortunately, I'm doing fine, and I have the house to myself for at least an hour, so I decide to make some lunch and settle in for a movie. After eating and stretching out on the couch, I'm feeling snoozy, but my phone buzzes.

Justice: Hey man. How goes married life? We haven't gotten to talk much at work.

"That's because we've both been in meetings and

running all over the NCR the last week," I grumble to myself and type out something similar to send to JJ.

I have genuinely loved being the commander of this unit, but it's starting to wear on me. I'm feeling restless, but not like I want to move. I think it's the other way around.

I'm feeling restless to... *not* move. To know I'll be able to stay here instead of getting sent off to some assignment where I have the neat opportunity to live in temporary housing in Kuwait or Jordan or Poland or Korea for the next year before beginning the next assignment. I've never begrudged the required moves because I've enjoyed them. And despite my marriage failing, I don't think I lost much.

I can't blame the Army for my divorce. The only people to blame are my ex-wife and me. I've never lied to myself about that, even if it has been hard to admit full-out.

Justice: Yeah. Exhausting week for sure.

I give this a thumbs up because I'm eloquent like that. It's not feeling great to look at the bright light of the phone screen. I'm ready to go back to the movie and maybe fall asleep for a little nap, but another message arrives.

Justice: So? How's it going? You guys getting along okay?

Are we? Great question. Most of me says yes. The other part of me says, *too well*.

Me: Doing just fine.

Justice: Very forthcoming of you.

Me: Shut it. This marriage is my business.

Justice: Funny how you say that like you didn't interfere with my marriage multiple times in the last year.

I don't try to stop myself from grinning at this.

Me: Yeah, but you got a best man out of it.

Justice: That I did.

I set my phone down and zone out to the movie until PB comes nosing around. He literally leans up on the cushion and sniffs all along my arm resting on the couch closest to him.

"Hello. Do I check out?"

Yes, I'm talking to him, but he's pretty endearing-looking. He's got a fluffy white and peachy-orange face, long whiskers and bright blue eyes, pink nose. He's honestly adorable and I'm not mad he's here, even if he did attack me the first time we met. I suppose accidentally crushing his tail under my combat boot in the same moment was more than payback.

I turn my palm up and he bobs along, sniffing to his heart's content, then shocks me with the odd scratch-lick of his tongue.

"Hey now, let's keep it PG there, fellow." I curve my hand and dare to pet him.

My heart glows when I hear the sound he makes—a warm, pleased hum that reminds me how much I like cats, and maybe, how soundless my life has been.

He moves his head, steering my hand one way and then the other as I stroke along the short fur between his ears. Finally, he drops down off his hind legs and I'm ready to see him saunter away, but instead, he makes a little sound I can't possibly describe and then he's on me, his pointy little feet right in my gut.

"Oh, hi. We're really getting friendly now, huh?"

He walks in a circle, then stops and wobbles before slumping down to rest fully on my chest, his paws between my pecs and his body stretched along my belly. His little rumble switch is turned back on as he tucks his face into his paws and closes his eyes.

I stare at him, oddly at a loss. I can't think of the last

time something has fallen asleep on me. It's been a long time, and it feels like... an honor.

"Guess we're friends now," I say, because apparently I'm happy to talk to him.

I've felt happy to talk to Andy, too.

This observation has me a little uncomfortable and far too aware I'm already messing this up. So instead of dwelling on that, I focus on the low hum of the cat's purr and a sense of peace and rest I haven't experienced in quite a while.

CHAPTER SIXTEEN

Andy

The waiter delivers our large bowl of guac and some chips and it's all I can do to keep my sigh inside.

"People, get yourself a man who looks at you like Andy looks at guacamole."

Grace laughs when I take a chip, scoop an unwieldy amount of guac, and chomp it in one bite.

After chewing and savoring the delicious flavors, I remind her, "You *do* have a man like that."

She grins. "I do, don't I?"

She's got a dreamy look on her face I can hardly stand because it's both so cute and I'm so jealous.

Wait.

What?

I'm not someone who longs for a partner. I really am not. I like having friends and I love love, but I haven't been gazing from a balcony singing "Some Day My Prince Will Come."

"What about you? Any chance you and Gruff will..." She wiggles her brows as though this completes her sentence.

Shaking my head, I shovel another chip to buy myself time. How honest do I want to be? How much should I share with her?

"You can tell me. Remember, if anyone understands your situation, it's me."

We didn't order margaritas because it's lunchtime and I want to be able to help Gruff later, and generally I don't love drinking during the day. But just now, I'm wishing with all of my fabulous cells that this was a dinner date and my buddies at the bar were about to deliver a Grinch margarita. 'Tis the season, after all, so I'll need to make that happen before it goes off-menu again in the new year.

"This feels like a conversation I need a margarita for," I admit, because at this point, I'm not sure how else to respond.

"Ah. Well. That's telling."

"Is it?" I don't know what it's telling of, but I guess I don't mind the idea that maybe she can see the situation more clearly than I can. "Why don't you tell me what you see because I'm a little confused."

The waiter brings our entrees and despite my messy feelings about Gruff, the beautiful plate of food in front of me is entirely uncomplicated.

Grace raises her water glass for a toast. "To fake marriages, real friends, and delicious food."

I touch my drink to hers and nod. "Amen."

After a few bites, during which I've been trying to identify how I actually feel about my life right now, Grace launches into her theory.

"I think you have genuinely disliked him until he came up with a solution to your problem that seems, from what you've said, to be a much better set-up for you than him."

I nod as I chew on my chimichanga, grateful she gets this part.

"I also think he's a very handsome man, and once you discover he's not all bad, it's hard to ignore that."

This is a reality I have reluctantly admitted to myself. He's always been attractive to me, but since I'm not the type to go for someone who comes off as a grade-A jerk, I never indulged in considering him as anything but JJ's grumpy boss and later friend. But now...

Her gaze is waiting when I raise my eyes to meet hers. "I will admit this has crossed my mind."

A smile flashes, but she hides it, almost like she thinks I'll spook if she lets me know she's happy with this discovery.

But here's the thing—I'm a sunshine. I'm happy-go-lucky for the most part, and I don't mind admitting it. Likewise, I am not opposed to confirming I like my husband. He's growing on me.

The alarming thing is just how fast.

"Okay, I just have to tell you. We're no longer spending one night at his parents' house in DC. We're now doing a four or possibly five-day trip to some resort in Vermont." Ah, yeah. There come the nerves.

My heartrate ticks up as the words settle between us, but Grace doesn't seem alarmed.

"And you're nervous about this."

I exhale, trying to calm myself. "Yes. I'm nervous

because I don't really know how it's going to be with his family. He's pretty closed off about them other than his desire to not be single for the holidays this year. *Noted.* But like... what does this mean? How do I act? I mean, his mother is intimidating as all get out by reputation alone and his dad is a retired senator. Like... what?"

Grace's expression softens. "You act like yourself. You're amazing, Andy."

I swallow, instantly struck with an abundance of feelings I don't like having. "I am. Sure. But... I'm just worried that being with me isn't going to do him any favors. And you're right—I like him. I'm not in love with the guy or anything, but even in the last twenty-four hours, I like him more than I would've dreamed I could six months ago. So that's great. But it also makes this part even more important. I don't want to just take what I can from him and divorce in six months. I want to help him, too."

Grace points her fork at me. "I get it. I really do. I felt the same about JJ. It seemed like I was getting the most out of our deal. And honestly? I was. But he needed me, and in the end..." Her smile turns into something a little dreamy. "In the end, we both needed each other."

My sigh must be too loud because she ducks her head to catch my eyes before speaking again.

"You don't ever have to love him, and you don't have to stay together. I hope it's clear that just because I lucked out that way, I'm under no illusions it will happen for you. But I also can't stand to hear you doubt yourself. You're amazing and there's no outward situation that'll change that."

Why am I getting emotional right now? I'm not this person. I'm not the kind who tears up or gets soppy. I'm... happy.

But part of this whole situation is because I've lost some

of my ability to power through negative feelings and be happy. And I hate it. More than anything, I hate the nagging feeling that I'm a burden.

"I am dreading what they'll think of me, but trying not to. I'm begging myself to just be content with where I am and not feel so upset that a year ago I was still on track to open my café before this Christmas, and now it's going to be at least six months before I'm ready, best case. I just feel like I've failed, and pretty soon, I'll be relying on Gruff to see me through post-surgery and—"

"Hey, hey. You think I'd let that man take care of you when I am an actual nurse? Heck no. You're not alone and listen." She grasps my wrist across the table. "You are not a burden. You are lovely. And occasionally needing someone's help isn't burdensome. Even if it was constant, you're still valuable. I know it's hard to believe, but I'm not blowing smoke."

Her wording cuts through the poor me feelings and I chuckle. "No? Well, that's good."

"Trust me. I'm a nurse. A really good one. And my husband's a lawyer."

I snort. "You're a weirdo is what you are."

She shrugs like this doesn't bother her a bit. "Maybe. But you are, too."

I grin, the tightness in my chest easing. "Touché."

We go on eating and move away from my sad feelings. I push past the fears of inadequacy and we talk about topics *other* than me and Gruff, and by the time I leave, I'm feeling better. Back on track and ready to make this a friendly agreement that has legs to walk us both to where we need to be in the next few months.

I'm fully determined to keep my eyes on the insurance prize. I can appreciate how handsome he is, how much I like him, but I don't need to *feel* things for the man. We won't even see each other much in the coming months, save the time with his family in a few weeks.

I have this crystal clarity up the nose, right until I walk into the house and see him asleep on the couch, cuddling with my cat.

CHAPTER SEVENTEEN

Andy

Before I melt into a puddle of adoration and ruin his lovely couch, Gruff's eyes flutter open.

"You're back." His voice is low and rough.

I like it way too much.

So much, especially paired with the absolute vision that is this man with my cat snoozing atop his belly, that I don't manage to respond. My mind has completely blanked and I'm floating in a pool of heart-melty bliss roughly the blue-gray color of Gruff's eyes.

Mmkay, well that may be a touch creepy, but it is not inaccurate.

"Grace okay?" he asks, his brow wrinkling.

And I am okay. I'm just fine. But then his large hand lifts and smooths from PB's head and down his body in a gentle pet that, yeah, makes me want to melt again.

I am a marshmallow dropped in steaming hot chocolate. I'm Olaf finally getting his chance to sunbathe.

Finally, I find words. "Um, yeah. Great. It was great. Have you eaten there? Tacos y Tacos?"

Yes, genius. Focus on the food and not how his hair's a little messy and it looks boyish and cute in a way you never anticipated.

"Once or twice. I remember it being good."

"It is good." I don't say it's exactly what I want when I think of Mexican food, and it's walking distance from his house, which makes it somehow even better. I decline to mention the plan already forming in my head to take him there and remind him just how good it is.

"I'm glad you had fun." He shifts, seeming uncomfortable.

Worry jabs me. "Is your migraine back?"

"No. I've just been in the same spot since right after you left." He stretches his neck side to side.

I'm surprised since I ended up being gone a good three hours by the time I had lunch with Grace and wandered around the Old Town shops for a while. "I'm glad you had a nice long nap."

He looses something that sounds like a whispered laugh. "I think I only actually slept for a half hour. I watched a movie and PB kept me company."

This, no surprise, delights me. "He did?" I round the couch and sink into the cushions a few feet from where the rumpled blanket covering him ends.

"He's been right here, anchoring me to the couch since I sat back down after a quick bite to eat. I haven't been able to move." He gives PB a stern look.

I hide my smile because I know this about myself—I'm too easily charmed by anything to do with cats. I could easily be talked into all manner of sins if one involved a cat.

Creepy white van pulls up and offers me a ride? Heck no! Creepy white van with a cat snoozing? Well, I *did* need a ride, now that you mention it.

Sketchy, broken-down building is the location my rideshare driver drops me? I'm turning right around. Unless there happens to be a sign that says "Cats Inside" and then I'm done for. Better go have a peek.

Person I find reprehensible by all accounts only to discover he or she has a cat they dote on? I'm a goner.

Basically, I have one weakness. It is my deep and abiding love of cats. And this man is playing on said weakness without even knowing it.

"He hasn't moved?" I ask, needing to confirm PB really has been on top of him for the last three hours.

"He repositioned about an hour ago—turned so he gave me the back end instead of his beady little eyes. I've considered getting up to stretch or get a snack or something, but haven't managed it because he's entirely unmotivated to surrender his napping place." His gaze stays on PB, who looks back for a moment then snuggles down into his spot and closes his eyes.

"Why didn't you just move?" I ask, still resisting the smile threatening at my lips.

He looks at me like I'm insane. "Because it's rude."

I snort-laugh. It is not a delicate thing, but this is too ridiculous. "Maybe? But he is a cat. He'll just find somewhere else to sleep. Napping is his life's work."

"That's rather callous coming from someone whose heart seems to bleed for these creatures." He strokes along PB's nose and up over the short fur at his forehead. I'm relieved when seconds later, he continues to speak and saves me from sounding like a jerk. "I mostly just didn't want to."

It's a bit weird for me to sit here watching him pet my cat so fondly, and I'm feeling more than a little caught off-guard by his... what? Animal positivity? Cat affinity? Softness?

I probably need to allow myself to think of how gentle he was with me the day he found me crying. If I keep that front and center, I won't be surprised by anything.

That day had nearly done me in, after all, and it led to this moment. I can feel the twinge of excited nerves filling my veins with a tragic amount of words that will be exiting my body one way or another in seconds, so I let loose now rather than running away and talking to myself, which I decide in a split-second decision is likely to make him think I really have lost my mind.

"So I think we need to talk about the time with your family because we're both going to be working a lot in the next few weeks and then I'm going to be nervous because I'm not a very fancy person and your family seems really fancy and I don't want to disappoint you because I'm just me and it's pretty basic over here. I want to do my best for you because you're already being so kind to me and I have my appointment with the specialist before we go to Vermont, and I just want to know what we need to do to make it worth all of this for you."

I suck in a breath, relief and mild horror hitting as I realize just how honest I've been.

His stunned expression eases, and there's a touch of a smile at the right corner of his mouth.

The unfortunate truth is, I've just noticed his mouth and how his beard seems to have grown in overnight, and now I'm imagining the scrape of his stubble against my lips, chin, cheek, neck...

"You're right. We do need to talk about it." His gaze falls to PB and he scruffles his fur again, finally pestering the furball enough that he opens a one eye and flicks his tail in warning.

"Peanut Butter, don't be crusty," I admonish.

Gruff's eyes shoot to mine. "PB is Peanut Butter? You named your cat after a condiment?"

I forgot I never mentioned the full names. Also, peanut butter is so much more than a condiment—has he even had it? "Peanut Butter and RJ is Raspberry Jelly."

He blinks. "That is... odd."

I laugh, strangely delighted by how perturbed he seems by the news. "First, I love peanut butter and raspberry jelly sandwiches. And second, when they were kittens, they started smashing together to sleep and in a weird way they looked like peanut butter and jelly."

He squints. "Your other cat is... red?"

"No. He's black and white, but in certain light he has a reddish hue. *Anyway*, less judging me for my cat names and more you telling me when we'll talk through our trip." I think the hint of a smile means he actually enjoys the names, but I can't be focusing any more on him liking things about me or my cats.

"Would you give me a few hours to get ahold of my mother and get a bit more information on the plan? She called right as my migraine was setting in and I don't remember if she told me much more than the dates."

"Of course. Yes. No rush, I just... we're here. And not working. I work tomorrow and on and off all week, and I know you do, too, so, yeah." *Stop talking, stop talking, stop talking.*

He sits up and slides back, muttering a low, "Sorry, fellow," when PB arches up, then dismounts with another flick of his tail as though he's been terribly inconvenienced by Gruff's insistence on being a human instead of an extension of the couch.

"Just let me know when you're ready," I say, then stand, energy pulsing through me that I need to funnel elsewhere or I'll continue to accost him with babble, and I don't want to cause another migraine.

"I will. Give me a few hours."

I scuttle down the hallway first, suspicious that if I walk behind him, I'll appreciate him in his lounge pants and soft T a little too much.

Instead, I'll lock myself in my room and work on... something I'll figure out soon, and not think about anything.

CHAPTER EIGHTEEN

Gruff

My mother answers on the second ring.

"You *are* alive. Thank you for deigning to notify me."

I don't muffle my long sigh. "Sorry. Looking at my phone screen wasn't the best idea yesterday and I've been taking it easy today to avoid a repeat."

She's quiet for a beat before she says, "I'm sorry, son. Was it awful?"

"Didn't last as long as some. I'm fine."

I can hear the things she's not saying from here as though she's lit them up on a marquee. *Are you sure you're okay? Should you go to the doctor? We can call in a favor...*

I have been to the doctor. My brain checks out with no larger concerns. Tension headaches that climb into migraines is the worst of it. Managing stress, exercising, avoiding crazy amounts of sugar, alcohol, and caffeine... I do what I can. But lately, I can't seem to escape the stress factor. Fortunately, my mother seems to understand that repeatedly insisting I see more specialists or take them up on calling in favors with famous Johns Hopkins docs or *whomever* won't help.

"Well, you're calling, so I'm guessing you have questions about Christmas."

God bless the woman for knowing her son and not making me ask. I would've. I can. But I am relieved not to feel like I'm begging for information. It may not make sense, but it's reality.

"Yes." I don't mention we aren't staying the whole time yet. It won't seem genuine since we've launched into a weekend, and I need it to seem like we're dropping a night thanks to Andy's or my work.

"We'll all arrive on the twenty second. We have a welcome cocktail hour, then I assume everyone will ski the next day until après ski at five." She continues on, detailing the list of days and times, including a Christmas Eve celebration and a Christmas morning brunch. It is, in theory, a nice schedule.

I wish I could look forward to it. The food will be impeccable, the skiing acceptable, even if it's not Silver Ridge or anywhere else in the Rockies where the snow is usually far superior to east coast skiing.

"We're so looking forward to having everyone together. I'll email you a copy of the itinerary so you have it. And did I tell you the Caldwells will be there?" She asks this even though she knows she didn't.

"You hadn't mentioned it. I'll be glad to see Janie and Chip." Yes, my cousin's name is Chip and he'll likely be an idiot, but he's a nice enough one at heart, and Janie is great. She'll love Andy. I hope the reverse will be true—Andy seems to be predisposed to like most people, so the odds are good.

"Yes. All of us together, and you newly married. It'll be great."

"Thanks for the details."

"Of course. I'm looking forward to getting to know Andy. I wish we had an opening for dinner before the trip, but you know how busy the holidays are."

"I do. We'll see you soon," I assure her, more than a little relieved we won't be seeing her any sooner than the twenty-second.

We say our goodbyes and I give myself a second to collect my thoughts. Movement to my right draws my eye and a cat comes in—the one I've never seen before. PB is a friendly fellow, and we've just leveled up our relationship after the marathon nap session, but this guy has been entirely MIA since move in days ago.

"Hello, RJ," I say, because I am demonstrably a man who talks to pets. It's interesting how I didn't know this until Andy moved in.

Now I know. I'm one of those people.

The cat is a small ball of black and white fur, the black laying like a blanket over him and his sides and belly a creamy white. His nose is working overtime, sniffing along the wall of books, the carpet, my shoes—

In a flash, the cat jumps three feet in the air, his tail doubling in width with his fur standing on end, and he's gone. There might as well be smoke and dust settling, he shot out of here so fast.

"Guess my running shoes are due for a freshen up," I chuckle to myself.

Andy peeks in then, grasping the doorknob.

"I'm so sorry. He hasn't ever left my room, so I didn't

worry about leaving the door open." She seems concerned for *me* rather than him.

"All good. He was just horrified by my shoes." I nod to the worn running shoes he found so deeply offensive.

She cracks up. "Oh, well. Yeah... I guess he's pretty honest."

She winks, and it sends a jolt of awareness through me. It's not sexual or even attraction, though. It's more like... longing.

But for what?

More moments like this, where we're both chuckling at her weird cats she named after sandwich ingredients? More of her tenderness and blushes and the way her eyes sparkle when she's amused or excited?

I am unlikely to get much more of those things than what she'd give a friend. And that's what I need to aim for here—friendship. Anything else is just not going to happen —not after my resounding failure at my first go at marriage and certainly not because that's not why we're here. Not what we agreed to.

"Do you want to get dinner in an hour or two? Maybe around six? Or, will you be too full?" I tack on the last thought when I realize it's only been a few hours since she had lunch.

She visibly startles but bites her lip through a smile that is just... lovely.

"I could eat. Sure. I'll just... see you in a bit." She pulls the door closed, disappearing and effectively ending our conversation, which is just as well. We'll have time at dinner.

At this point, I realize this will be our first date. Or, fake date, I suppose. We could talk through things here, but we've never been out together before now since we've hardly spent any time together.

We'll need to be convincing in Vermont, so this is a good way to start. It's for the sake of my family's perception of us. If we've literally never been on a date, how are we going to convince everyone we're blissfully in love and happily married?

We won't.

Exactly.

So, we'll practice up for the Christmas trip.

And not for any other reason.

CHAPTER NINETEEN

Andy

I am sitting across from Wilson Gruff in a dimly lit bistro with soft instrumental Christmas music playing, twinkle lights strung around the windows facing a quaint street, and it feels nothing short of completely romantic.

It is also totally fine and no big deal. I am definitely not nervous, and I was not flittering around my room like a crazy woman half an hour ago before he knocked on the bedroom door, and I am not even remotely already struggling to hold back the verbal deluge of nonsense threatening to crash down on this quiet moment between us.

Oh. Wait.

Yeah.

I don't know why I've decided to focus on the intense attraction I feel to him *now* of all times, but it's there. Probably thanks to my conversation with Grace, or maybe because he was sweet to not one but *both* of my cats in the span of less than an hour.

Honestly, napping with and petting PB was enough to clench the deal. But when he knocked, freshly showered and his hair was a little wet and curling over his forehead in the most boyish way, it sent me straight back to junior high when I had a crush on Bobby Townsend and couldn't stop giggling.

He's wearing a crisp button-down shirt in a hunter green that is both very attractive and pleasingly seasonal with jeans and nice leather shoes I didn't look too closely at for fear I'd seem like I was checking him out.

Let's be clear: I was. One hundred percent checking out the way his butt looked in the jeans. His shoulders filled out the shirt, his stubble did *not* get shaved, and I'm thrilled about it. I checked him out, then did it again, and I can't stop focusing on small details now while his focus is on the menu in front of him.

He's got a scar that runs through his left eyebrow. It's only noticeable when he raises his brows, and I have the brutally vivid fantasy of sitting on his lap and tracing the tip of my finger over that arch, then leaning in to kiss where the scar juts up toward his temple.

It is not okay. Really ridiculously not okay to the highest order. Someone tell my brain to stop with the nonsense because I cannot be sitting here thinking about such things. That is a one-way ticket to heartbreak city and I have no interest in moving again, thank you very much.

At least not for the next six months...

Right. *Right.* Because then, I will move out of his perfect house.

See? Intrusive thoughts about how much I like every-thing about him are killing me. I need Grumpy Gruff back and then it'll all be fine. I'm sure he'll show up any time now...

"Any idea what you'd like to order?"

"I—no. I—" I reach for my water and guzzle down half of the glass.

"What's wrong?" he says, his tone closer to the pushy version of himself than I've had in a while which is, frankly, helpful at the moment.

"I just realized this is kind of our first date. And that's so weird because we are *married*, Gruff, and I don't know what to do with that because it's not a normal marriage but I'm also not the kind of woman who grew up dreaming of getting married and yet I definitely dreamed of love and that's not what we have here and—" I suck in a long breath, and my brain finally catches up with my mouth enough to halt me completely.

He waits a beat before prompting, "And? Don't leave me hanging."

"And I'm nervous."

His stern gaze is a spotlight on every little twitch and tremble. We're only a few feet apart with the small two-person table between us.

"Why are you nervous? With me?"

I mine myself, wondering whether that is the issue. Thankfully, I don't think it's him. Yes, he gives me the zings, but it's not just that.

"No. Not with you. I trust you as much as is possible, or I wouldn't have moved into your house. But I know this matters to you and I don't want to mess it up." There.

And as obvious as it is since I did move in with the man, I'm shaken by how true my words are. I trust him as much as I've trusted almost anyone, maybe with the exception of Grace. Even then, I trusted him with the secret reality of my debt and medical issues in a way I couldn't burden her with. I think somewhere deep down, I trusted he would be honest with me, maybe even gruff and rude, but he wouldn't hurt me.

It's... dangerous, this realization. I'm already vulnerable enough having spewed out the truth between us. I can't let the facts cause an avalanche effect in me. Just because I tend not to open up, and I keep unzipping right down to my bones for him doesn't mean... anything.

His serious expression doesn't break, even when the waiter approaches. I order an appetizer for dinner because I did my very best to stuff myself at lunch, and in this I did not fail, but I need something in front of me for this dinner.

Gruff orders a salad, then a salmon dish that sounds great and I wish I was hungry enough to get for myself. *Alas.*

The waiter leaves us, and I stare where my plate will be and try to recall what I just ordered—it's a little cheesy puff pastry thing with cranberries and walnuts I've already forgotten the name of and it sounded delicious, but my appetite is now gone completely.

"You can't mess anything up, Andy."

My head snaps up at the sound of my name. "I can't?"

"There's nothing *to* mess up. We've got some details to work out, and I agree that we need to get to know each other so our relationship is more believable, but if anything goes wrong, it won't be your fault."

His darkened eyes in this low lighting are basically hypnotizing me. He's Jafar's staff with swirling eyes, but he's not an evil sorcerer. He's just being kind and handsome and somehow tapping into the biggest fear I have—that I'll ruin something for him when he's doing so much for me.

"I appreciate the sentiment. But I think if we're hanging

out with your family and they see us like this, they're going to know we're not really married." I don't know exactly why, but my cheeks heat.

He studies me, the intensity of his gaze a heavy thing. It's one of those weighted lead drapes that goes over you before you get dental X-rays—odd, a bit unnerving, and weirdly comforting.

"We've got time. Just under three weeks until we're with them. So we'll use our time wisely."

Some part of me wishes he'd make light of it needing to seem real. It'd be so much easier if it didn't actually matter that his family believes us. Or better yet, if he could just toss out an, "Of course they'll believe it's real!" and we'd call it good.

But reality is clinging to both of us—to my body where my stupid parathyroid is... doing or not doing whatever it's supposed to do, and to his life where he's staring down a family reunion he felt strongly enough about that he *married* me. So, yeah, we're already doing enough pretending. Might as well be honest about what we need to make this work.

"True. We have a little time."

He nods. "I won't be traveling again and work usually slows down at least a week before the holidays. So we'll just have to go out and... do whatever couples do."

I take this in for a moment, but his expression is so endearingly removed from *whatever couples do*, it tickles me. A laugh tumbles out, and his lips thin.

"I'm not laughing at you. You just seem so baffled by that fill in the blank." I clear my throat and lower my voice to a deeper timbre. "We'll do whatever couples do." I chuckle again.

"This is funny?"

His skepticism is real. This is the old Gruff—unamused and completely blank, save mild disdain for me and my silliness.

I clear my throat in earnest this time. "Sorry. No. I wasn't trying to be a jerk. I just... I'm still nervous. And I haven't dated someone in a few years, so I honestly can't actually fill in the blank well either. I'm a homebody for the most part, anyway."

There's silence between us and restaurant sounds cover it well enough—the music softly playing "I'll Be Home for Christmas," the hum of conversation, and the tink tink of fork tines and knives on plates. I'm scrambling internally, fully aware that any second, another deluge of nonsense is going to come out, and at this rate it'll be digging a deeper hole between us, when he saves me from myself.

"I will admit, I don't know either. I've been divorced for five years and separated before that, and I haven't dated since."

This truth spreads between us like spilled milk and I can't hide my disbelief.

"Seriously? You haven't dated since your divorce?"

Because honestly, how? I mean, sure, a year ago if you'd asked me, I would've cracked a joke about how his personality probably repelled most prospective partners in a twenty-foot radius, but I know better now.

He might seem grumpy and the very definition of his last name, but he's a decent human being. That cannot be overestimated because it is not all that common. And he's thoughtful and capable in ways I can personally vouch most men are not.

He's gruff, yes, but he's also generous and accommodating and...

"I have not."

And withholding, apparently, but I never said he was perfect. "I'm just kind of amazed. I mean, you're so..."

"I had no desire to date when I had no desire to remarry." He says this like it's the most obvious statement of fact in the history of man.

I'm processing this as the waiter sets down my appetizer and his salad. We thank him, and I press the potentially awkward subject.

"Okay, maybe you didn't want to get married again, but... companionship? Or... um, you know, any other needs a person might have?" I'm not saying it outright but like, he knows what I mean, right?

He's stabbed several pieces of his salad—which looks fabulous and I wish I'd gotten it, by the way—but stops with a forkful of food resting at the side of his plate.

"Are you asking me whether I've slept with anyone in the last five years, Andy?"

I flush hot instantly. I am likely years away from perimenopause but *this* must be what women talk about when they mention hot flashes. I am a thousand degrees from the inside, a fuse lit and burning outward, skin on fire and I wouldn't be surprised if my eyelashes are singed off.

Also, why must he say my name? It makes these exchanges so... personal.

Sensual?

I don't know but I'm not sure I'm mature enough for this.

He clearly sees me floundering and one side of his mouth slides up in what I can fully admit is the sexiest little half-smile I've ever seen on the man.

Probably any man, if I'm honest.

This does not help me.

I stab wildly at my plate and shove something in my

mouth because I will not be answering his question, no sir, no ma'am, no can do, thanks.

Not that I'm not curious, but no.

I can't admit I am, or that I genuinely can't imagine he's just not dated or seen or kissed or *anythinged* anyone in well over five years.

It feels like a waste, frankly.

His smile grows and my heartrate quadruples because I suspect, as I chew a too-large bite of puff pastry and brie and something else I can't parse out right now, he can read my mind.

I wait for him to speak or walk back the question—anything to alleviate the flames now torching my chest cavity and blazing in my brain, but he doesn't.

In fact, he takes a cocky sip of his beer, then slowly chews his salad like a sophisticated adult man having a conversation with another person and not like a teen girl masquerading as an adult and I realize my very fatal error in all of this.

For as taciturn as he has been, his generosity fooled me. I got comfortable with him when he had his migraine and he was sweet to my cats.

And I forgot that this man is actually incredibly dangerous.

CHAPTER TWENTY

Gruff

I don't think of myself as a bad man, but the sweet burn of pleasure I'm getting from the blush in Andy's cheeks, and the way she's not quite looking me in the eye, makes me second-guess.

It's not right to enjoy someone's discomfort, is it?

No. Obviously not.

And yet.

She is ridiculously uncomfortable, and I can't help the smile still pulling at my lips. I have half a mind to let this anguish go on until she has another one of her verbal oil spills and reveals more of herself, but after another minute or two of tension wafting from her, I decide to let her off the hook.

"I can answer that question if you really want me to, but I suspect maybe you don't." I'll admit I don't mind the idea that she's curious about my dating life—all aspects of it.

Our gazes are hooked into one another's. We hang there in the moment, like her answer will change things between us even though of course it won't. My fingers form a fist and press into my thigh to counteract the impulse telling me to slide the strands of hair that've fallen in front of her face away and tuck them behind her ear.

She lets out a rolling sigh and blinks, breaking the spell. "Thank you, but no. I think I probably shouldn't know *that*. I mostly just mean you're super handsome and successful and I don't get how you—" She presses her lips together and her eyes close slowly like the curtain over a stage.

I laugh because she's adorable and so delightfully honest. She has already surprised me several times, and it just keeps getting better. She's not demanding truth from me without offering it up for herself, and I don't know why this is a surprise, but I like it.

I'm eating it up, in fact.

"I'm super handsome, huh?" This is the closest I've come to flirting with someone in... I don't know how long. A very long time, for sure. It's also the most fun I've had with anyone in far too long.

Her pretty mouth drops open, and I've stunned her into silence. It's miraculous, but I'm disappointed because I want her to keep revealing herself.

Her gaze narrows and she laughs. "You are... you're sneaky."

"Me? I don't think I've ever been called sneaky."

She shakes a finger at me. "You are. You seem all grumpy and quiet, but you're actually a sneaky flirt."

I'm laughing again, and her answering smile injects a levity and joy to this moment that is almost painful in its foreignness.

"Forgive me," I say, a hand pressed over my heart.

Her expression shifts to one I can only describe as inordinately pleased. "Forgiven. And now, instead of talking about dating, how about you tell me about your career? I'm guessing this is something I should know about you, so... take it away."

She's deftly shifted the focus, and I move with her.

"I'm a colonel in the Army. Active duty. I've been at this duty station for two years and my change of command is coming up. I will likely have orders for my next move by mid-January." My heart sinks just saying it out loud.

The shock on her face is as clear as any other emotion she displays, but this one pinches me.

"I had no idea you were moving. How soon?"

Is she worried I won't fulfill my part of our bargain? I drew up the contract precisely for this reason.

"Likely late spring to early summer. It is possible I could find another position in NCR but—"

"Sorry, NCR?" She tilts her head to the side, then slides another bite of her appetizer between her lips.

I will not focus on her lips or mouth. I will answer her question.

"National Capital Region. Sorry, that's more military speak. I guess people usually say Nova instead?" Northern Virginia being the more common term, military and government employees tend to refer to NCR since it could include areas surrounding DC when discussing duty stations and job assignments.

"Gotcha. Okay, sorry. Please continue." She waves a hand at me as if to say, "the floor is yours." My eyes catch on her bright red and white candy cane striped nail polish as she makes the flourish.

"Not much more to say. I've had a very successful career.

I'm proud of it. But—" I search for the right way to put it, though that's a pipe dream since I haven't found a way to explain what I feel to myself as it is. "I don't know. I'm tired."

I reach for my beer, and she finishes a bite of her food before asking, "How many times have you moved?"

I tally it up in my mind. "Fifteen times, not including short term moves for schools. I had a six-month stint somewhere—stuff like that. And not including deployments, obviously."

Her eyes widen and something shifts in her expression, but this one I can't read. She typically broadcasts so clearly, but I don't know what it is hiding there behind her eyes now.

Maybe she hates that I'm a soldier. Some people really do disdain the profession, but this often comes from either a bad personal experience, or a misunderstanding. That, or sweeping generalizations, which is always the best way to understand the world, isn't it?

"That's incredible." She seems to genuinely mean it.

Though so far, I haven't found anything she's not genuine about.

"It has been a good life," I say somewhat woodenly. I've never felt resentful of moving—always had a certain pride in my career. Maybe it's facing the family reunion, or this sense in me that I should have something else... I don't know what, but I'm edgy.

"I've never lived anywhere but Virginia," she says, an air of marvel in her tone.

"Really? Have you ever wanted to move out of state?" It's hard to imagine never living elsewhere, though until I went to college, I'd only ever lived here, too.

"Sort of? I moved out of my small town for college and

then ended up here working and have been here ever since."

"And do you like it?" Maybe I'm pushing too hard, but I have to wonder. Her life has been diametrically different than mine—not an unusual occurrence when less than one percent of the country serves in the military, but still.

She finishes a bite and sets her fork down. "It probably seems crazy for someone like you, but I do. I love this area, especially Alexandria. It feels like home to me."

Her eyes hold mine, then bounce away to flit around the restaurant.

"I've enjoyed other places for sure. Wiesbaden, Germany was gorgeous. South Korea is incredible. Loved being near Seattle for a bit and in the Rockies at Carson. But DC's always been home." And I've never felt it more keenly than now, when I'm mentally preparing to get orders to the next place.

"You grew up *in* DC, but you live out here in Old Town?" she asks, leaning one elbow on the table and a cascade of her hair falls over her shoulder.

My eyes follow the movement of the bright pink tips of her hair that slide over her collar bone and down, down, until it's hanging by her ribs. My gut tightens.

"Much to my mother's dismay, yes. She doesn't understand why I'm not in DC proper, but I bought this place years ago when I did a tour at the Pentagon, and I love it. I'll be sad to leave it," I admit, and feel that in my gut.

"It is seriously so beautiful. I'm amazed at your good taste." Her eyes widen. "I mean, that's insulting, but I just don't have that kind of style, so I'm impressed when anyone does, not just you."

I chuckle low, enjoying her explanation and the way her fingers are sifting through the last few inches of her hair.

"I can't take the credit. That's actually my cousin, Janie's, doing. She's an interior designer and I got a great family discount. You'll meet her in Vermont." Janie will love Andy and she'll make the time bearable.

"That's amazing. I love everything about your house. It's beautiful." Her expression shifts and she bites her lip, then leans back as the waiter takes her plate. They swap my salad out with my entrée before she continues.

"I wanted to mention that you should really sleep in your own bed."

I stare at the beautifully prepared salmon and blink once, twice. What I'm hearing is *you should sleep with me in your bed* and I know that's not what she's saying, but I can't seem to make sense of what she *is* saying.

"Uh, well, uh—"

"I just feel bad. Your study is beautiful, and it's a lovely gesture to give me the primary bedroom, but I'd prefer if we switch." Her eyes have somehow grown larger and more earnest.

Mercifully, before I say something completely idiotic and make her uncomfortable, her meaning finally clicks. "Ah, right. No, no. I'm perfectly content in the library and I'm happy for you to have space. You and the cats enjoy it while you're living there."

Her smile brightens on the surface, but I could swear her eyes dim. I can't be sure why, and I want to ask, but she changes the subject, asking more about my family, so I roll along with her.

By the end of the evening, I've come to two conclusions.

First, I like Andy Barnes, and it won't be feigning interest when we're with the family.

And second, I let her get away with shifting the focus back to me, or maybe I was just a self-focused jerk enough that I still don't know much about her. How'd she end up working at a coffee shop, and what happened after college? And why does she not have an actual boyfriend?

Now that we'd agreed we need to get to know each other to convince my family, I'm not going to hold back from asking next time we're together.

CHAPTER TWENTY-ONE

Andy

The line at the register is doubling by the minute.

Soon, it reaches the door and snakes around the two fake Christmas trees we have as a part of our little entryway display, blocking the exit.

Corbin, our newest employee, is a lovely kid, but he's also more than a little dense, and putting him on the register during the morning rush on a Monday feels a little like seeing a problem coming from a mile away and doing nothing to stop it.

I typically act as manager during the week, and the owner keeps his hands off, but this morning, Paul Jenkins, owner and operator of Alex Brews, beat me here and was showing his lovely college-aged nephew who's home for the holidays the ropes.

And that's great. Except Paul rarely actually works the register since he has a full staff and three managers on rotation, so his lessons, plus Corbin's sense of absolute negative urgency, is creating an actual nightmare.

I'm eying the line for regulars and starting their drinks because I already know what they'll have. Courtney gives me wide eyes from her spot at the espresso machine as she pulls shots and I just nod.

"I'm giving him thirty seconds to get through this person and then I'm handing him off to Pedro at eight the minute he walks in. What I'll do with him for the next fourteen minutes..." I flare my eyes at her.

She rolls her eyes and shakes her head, clearly as annoyed as I am that Paul suggested he take a turn on the register today of all days. That said, Corbin did indicate he has experience with customer service and food service, but I feel like maybe this isn't true.

When customers start shifting around and someone shouts, "Can someone help him?" I scuttle to the rescue.

Shan is doing their best on the register next to Corbin and gives me a look far too similar to the one Courtney just did. I mouth "I know" and slide up next to Corbin just shy of brushing his shoulder.

"Hi there. I'm going to ask you to shadow me for the next ten, and then I'm going to have you shadow Pedro." I smile at the kid.

He's nineteen or twenty and seems nice enough, but I wonder if he's on something because he's rather slow to respond. He blinks, then ducks his head in a doofy nod. "Cool. I can just shadow her." He turns and points at Courtney.

She doesn't have to turn for me to see that if I send him over to watch her, I will also need to dial emergency services because I will have been murdered by a woman doing the job of two baristas.

"Nah, let's have you stick with me for now, okay? You can watch Shan, too. We're both experts." I wink at him like this is all fun, but I'm also ringing the next customer up and writing the order out on a cup.

"Right on," Corbin says, and I flash him a smile that I soon shift to the next person in line.

I take orders, slide cups down the line to Court, and we go on like this. I haven't glanced up to take in the line, but it's dwindling, which means Shan and I are making progress, and Pedro will alleviate the pinch all the more. Of course, the day he's coming in late is a crush like this.

"You know, you're handling this like a pro. Just wanted to say, way to manage the insanity here," the man who steps up to the register says.

"Thanks so much. What can I get you?" I ask, pen in hand.

He gives me his order and pays, but then doesn't move. I look up, customer service smile in place, and find he's staring at me with... well, with a surprisingly handsome face. He's about my age give or take, looks like he's heading into the city for work in a suit and a nice wool overcoat, and he's got this charming smile on his face.

"Name for the order?" I ask, sharpie ready.

"Andrew." He smiles a very pretty smile. "And you?"

Unaccustomed to the even exchange, I laugh. "Andy."

He beams. "Ah, Andrew and Andy. Perfect."

I focus on writing his name. He's definitely flirting with me, and I don't mind it, but it's also not appropriate on a few levels, primarily because I'm married. Granted, I'm not wearing a ring so he's not being a creep.

I slide his cup over and hand him his receipt.

"Sorry to hold anyone up, but I just have to ask if you're

available?" He shifts closer and ducks his head to speak a little quieter. "I'd love to take you out."

"And I'd love for you to stop hitting on my wife."

The man in front of me startles, as do I, when Wilson Gruff steps forward and glares at him with a set jaw and the fiercest eyes I've ever seen. *Yikes.*

But also... holy crap. He just *my wife'*d me and it's kind of doing things to me. The customer—Andrew—holds up both his hands.

"Sorry, man. I had no idea. She's not wearing a ring, and I—" His eyes widen and he takes a giant step to his right, hands still raised.

I'm watching Gruff, and he's silenced the man with only a look—rather, a glare so vicious and full of promise, poor Andrew didn't even bother finishing his sentence. He's wearing his uniform so he's sporting the dappled greens, tans, and browns of what he calls his "OCP" uniform, the more casual camouflage look, and yet still contextually startling and lethal-looking. Paired with his stoney expression and the storm cloud demeanor, it's certainly more intimidating than a nice suit—sorry, Andrew.

"Well, hello," I say, because I am experiencing an out-of-body delight in this moment. I'm practically hovering over my own shoulder, witnessing the towering man I recently married mean-mugging a customer and I'm certain anyone watching can see I'm eating it up.

Gruff doesn't take his eyes away from Andrew, so I reach for his hand where it rests on the counter. The contact, my palm against his knuckles, draws his gaze to me.

He takes me in as though Andrew had touched me or harmed me in some way.

"He was just being friendly," I say, starting to wonder

whether he's actually upset about what just happened or if something else is going on.

"He was flirting. He asked you out."

I pull back and grab a coffee cup, readying my sharpie. "He had no idea I'm married and oddly enough, I don't greet every person I meet with that fact."

He glowers.

"Are you okay?" I lower my voice even though Andrew has moved well away. "This feels like a lot considering our situation."

His jaw flexes, and all delight at his *my wife* has fled.

"I won't tolerate infidelity, even between us."

My heart sinks. "I would never."

He's on edge and it makes me a little sick... I'm all too aware of his reaction and how it might mean he has a history with circumstances that were suspicious. But right when I'm about to ask if he can give me a minute and I'll take a break and make clear I'd never *ever* cheat on him, his expression smooths.

"I know. I don't know everything about you yet, but I know that."

His darkened eyes flicker back and forth between mine and I wish with every fiber of my existence that we were alone somewhere so I could hug him, or kiss him, or—well, no. That'd be a slippery slope.

His certainty of me is heartening, even if all of this will absolutely require more discussion. I mentally restrain the part of me begging to hassle him about this and ask, "What can I get you?"

I could swear something flickers behind his eyes, and then he orders a black coffee.

Ugh. This man. I slide the cup down the line and close my register for a second, resisting the urge to call out something insane like a matcha mocha caramel frap like I would in months past when Gruff ambled in just begging to be pestered.

"You good for a minute? I'm going to take a break," I say to Shan, who nods. There's one person at the register, and no one else, so I grab Gruff's cup, fill it up, and notch my head to the side. Since he's been watching my every move through all of this, he follows.

I slip into the café proper past the service counter and he's there, darkened gaze and slightly less dark mood greeting me.

"Your coffee, sir." I say sir because he's in his uniform today and he looks remarkably sexy and also intimidating. I can see why Andrew instantly backed down. I also cannot blame myself for *needing* a moment with him.

"Sorry," he says, probably referencing the whole scene at the register.

"You can claim me. That's allowed." I shrug a shoulder like having this man do such a thing isn't still causing a mild arrhythmia.

"You need a ring. I can't believe I'm just now thinking of it."

I tip my head to one side. "You probably do, too. I'm afraid I can't intimidate anyone if they're flirting with you."

His eyes narrow. "People don't flirt with me."

I smile, because he's too serious. He was far more relaxed last night at dinner... and this morning, he's in Gruff mode to the max.

"Well, I'll flirt with you then. We'll swap rings, and then we'll flirt with each other. Deal?" I sound like an absolute raving idiot, but I'm okay with it. I'm in a *great* mood today, especially now that he's played out one of my favorite romance tropes and we're through the morning rush.

His brows knit, but then he surprises me. He steps close, and I realize he's another inch or so taller in his tan combat boots. He reaches for my hand and grasps it, somehow with strength and gentleness. My heartrate kicks up at the feel of his rough palms, and I'm looking straight into his brutally handsome face when he says, "Deal."

Then he leans down and drops a kiss to my cheek, the closest we have ever been, and then he's gone, striding away with his long legs in a uniform that looks really good on him and a gait that says, "I will crush you if you get in my way."

I chuckle under my breath and my fingers drift to the place where his lips pressed into my cheek.

It's so, so stupid, but I've now confirmed it.

I have a crush on my fake husband.

CHAPTER TWENTY-TWO

Gruff

Her smile is beaming in a way that should seem fake but is hitting me just right.

Actually, it seems everything she does hits me that way. It's like ever since I saw that customer hitting on her and I became a feral beast ranting about not talking to my wife, I can't go back. Something flipped in me, and I had this overwhelming need to proclaim her *mine*.

But to be fair, she hadn't done anything wrong, and in truth, I couldn't blame what's his face for trying. Andy is beautiful and friendly and has this efficient, thoughtful way about her at the coffee shop. If I wasn't a social hermit uninterested in dating, maybe I would've asked her out months ago.

Ha. No.

And yet, here we are in my living room with her gazing at me and making me feel things.

I turn away. "You can stop with the cheesy smiles." I fail to sound properly grumpy.

"I'm just... too happy. Like, I'm so happy I want to dance in circles and fling glitter bombs."

"Uh, no, thank you," I say, certain that if I ever encounter a glitter bomb in real life, it will absolutely come from her.

She launches herself at me and wraps her arms around my waist, squeezing and releasing before I can move to do anything. "Thank you."

"I'm not sure getting a Christmas tree warrants so much happiness, but okay. Happiness noted. And you're welcome." Every place she touched me still feels *better* than it did before contact, a reality which I stoutly ignore because I won't survive this situation if I don't.

"It does, though! You got us a real tree." She says this with so much enthusiasm, she's almost yelling though her volume hasn't increased.

"You were there, too," I correct.

With a shake of her head, she approaches me, a medium-sized storage bin in hand. "You could've insisted on using the fake one you already had. Instead, you got a real tree."

I scowl. "You said your cats would die if we used the fake tree. That hardly seemed like something I could insist on. I'm not a monster."

Though I wouldn't have. It's not like I made her beg.

She chuckles, her bright white teeth shining and perfect. She has one of those mouths made to smile—pretty lips that frame her straight teeth her parents must've paid dearly for via orthodontia, or maybe she's just genetically blessed. I clear my throat and take the box from her when I notice her adjusting her grip to ease the weight off her right wrist.

"They do tend to try to kill themselves by eating fake greenery and tinsel. The vet bill two years ago the first time I had a fake tree was enough to send the message that the boys demand fresh spruce." She surrenders the box, a touch of a wrinkle between her brows, but then scampers to the door when the bell rings.

I set the box on the couch and follow her, sliding the delivery guy a five as a meager tip, and take the tree from her before she hurts herself. It's eight feet at least.

"Oh my gosh, it already smells amazing."

The cats are skittering around, eying the wrapped tree like it has arrived from an alien planet and was sent to murder them. PB is most aggressively stalking his future prey and RJ has disappeared down the hallway to Andy's room.

Andy's room. It's a funny thought considering it's my bedroom, and yet having her in there feels exactly right. Unsettling when I recall how tired of having to share any space with my ex I became, but that mostly resulted from the knowledge that she not only fell out of love with me, if she ever did fall in love with me in the first place, but actively disliked me in the end.

We work together to settle the tree into the stand. She screws it into place and goes to get water while I snip the twine keeping the limbs wrapped up.

PB parries forward with one paw out and slaps at the dangling string, then skitters back, predator eyes wide and unblinking.

"It won't hurt you. You'll end up hurting it if you're not careful," I explain quietly, not sure I want Andy knowing how much I talk to her cat.

"He's right, PB. And no climbing." Andy's voice is right there, and clearly, she heard me.

"Climbing?" I watch as she goes to one knee and pours water into the base of the stand from a big cup, then reattaches the decorative collar that will also keep the cats out. I make a note to show her where the small watering can is.

"Yeah. Last year, this guy felt compelled to get to know every inch of the tree. He knocked it over twice and almost got really hurt." She sets the cup down and runs a hand over her cat.

"Do we need to anchor it better?"

"No. I only have the boring decorations so, as long as you don't mind, he won't be lured in. Nothing shiny or noisy or... well, anything." She takes the lid off the container and reveals a plethora of felt and fabric ornaments.

"Those are nice."

It slips out before I check myself. It doesn't matter, really. They *are* nice. And she can't know how much I like them instantly, the homey reds, greens, grays, and whites of the palette she's clearly chosen. She can't know it's the inverse of the fake tree and gold and silver presentation my ex-wife preferred. A beautiful combination, but not personal.

These little scraps shaped into birds and angels and candy canes might be homemade or store-bought, but they are deeply personal. They are selected to keep her cats safe, and to celebrate, and because, I just know it, she liked them.

"Are they okay? Not particularly fancy, but—"

"I really like them," I insist.

She hides her smile but that expressive face of hers tells me anyway. Soon enough, she's got Nat King Cole's classic album playing and the fireplace lit and we've painstakingly wrapped two strands of lights around the tree—well, I did while she kept PB from repeated attacks from all corners of the room. To be fair, the lights do have an enticing little slither so I can't blame the fellow.

Now we're hanging little felt ornaments all over the tree and it feels good. I'm unaccustomed to the sensation so I can't quite put a finger on it, but this, with her, feels inexplicably good.

"What's your favorite Christmas movie?" She's stretching to reach a tall branch and without thinking, I set my hands on her waist to steady her from behind.

I feel and hear the small intake of breath. She slips the loop over a branch and lets the ornament hang down, easing back onto her heels. I release her with enough reluctance to signal an internal reprimand.

That's enough of that, man.

"Uh, *Die Hard.*"

She laughs loudly. "Ho Ho Ho." We finish the line together. "It is classic, even if I don't love it categorized as a Christmas movie."

I can't explain why I like her answer, but I do. She hasn't outright rejected my choice, nor has she fully allowed that it's a true Christmas movie. "The entire setting is a Christmas party. There's friendship. Romance. Good triumphing over evil. And John McClane learning about the spirit of Christmas. What more does it require to be an official Christmas movie?"

She laughs again, such an unleashed, joyous sound, it hits a target in my chest I hardly knew existed.

"Ridiculous, but well-stated. For me, I'd take a bit more romance." Her face softens as she hangs the last ornament. "*Love, Actually* will always be mine, even though half the timelines are horribly sad and it hasn't aged perfectly."

I don't recall the movie in detail. "Would you like to watch it?"

"Never a question that needs to be asked."

With a chuckle, I gather up a few pieces of trash and eye PB where he's sitting on the arm of the couch, Christmas lights reflecting in his beady little eyes. I recall her recounting how he and RJ both got themselves tangled up in the lights she hung up in her own room—and of course she hung Christmas lights in her room.

I want to see them.

Also I need to stop that nonsense.

"Be good," I tell PB, then toss the remote to Andy. "Cue it up. I've got to grab something."

My heart is beating faster by the time I return and find her nestled into the couch, both PB and RJ circling the blanket she's wrapped up in ready to hunker down with her. I take a seat a little closer to her than normal and hand her the small velvet box.

"This is overdue. I apologize I didn't have it for you the day we got married. I hope you'll feel comfortable wearing it." My throat is dry, and my breathing is shallow.

"Oh," she says on a whisper and tilts the box open to reveal the rings—a wedding band the jeweler called an eternity band with small circle-cut diamonds all the way around and an engagement ring with a tear-drop-shaped diamond, both set in rose gold. "*Oh.*"

"Good *oh*?" I ask like an idiot, because as often as I think I can read her, I can't right now and it's imperative I understand what she's thinking. It's unique and maybe a little *too* different. Maybe she would've liked platinum. Maybe a princess cut? I don't know enough about these things but this set just felt like her. "Too much?'

Her mouth drops open, eyes still on the rings. It's

perhaps a touch more ostentatious than she might choose, but fueled by the events at the coffee shop earlier, I wanted something that would be... visible.

"It's just so gorgeous. I mean, are you sure?" Her gaze meets mine and hooks into me.

"Of course. If you like it, it's yours."

Keep it however long you want, a voice whispers in my head. Thankfully, I do not say this aloud like a weirdo.

Her smile cracks, pulling at one side of her mouth before spreading wide. "It's gorgeous. Thank you."

With a surprisingly steady voice, I ask, "May I?"

She nods, completely still save her one hand surrendering the box.

I remove the rings and take her left hand in mine, then slowly work the rings over her ring finger. There's a tightness in my chest but it's not bad—it's not stress. It's an alien sensation I suspect is a mix of longing and maybe even grief. Like nostalgia for something I've never experienced.

For her, and this, and us wrapped in permanence instead of punctuated by a ticking clock I hear more incessantly every day.

When her arms reach for me, sliding over my shoulders and hooking around my neck, the frenetic worry bouncing around my body and mind settle, that ache easing. She squeezes me tight, pulling me in for a hug. Her head tucks in and she's genuinely holding me in a way I know I'll think about later. I press my hand to the center of her back and indulge the impulse to press a hand to the back of her head, too. A moment to cradle her, comfort her, *keep her,* that errant voice whispers again, and then we release.

"I need to get you a ring," she says, blinking rapidly as she pulls away and, I think, swipes under her left eye.

I hold up my left hand showing a black tungsten ring

that is boring but functional. "I went ahead and got one today. I hope you don't mind." She doesn't need to be spending money on such things.

She grins. "Not at all. Just as long as we're both claimed." She wiggles her eyebrows.

I nod as though her wanting me claimed is a joke, and I think this is all funny.

But that voice, incessant as it is, won't stop saying what I know is true. Through the movie, and as I take in the stillness of the night when the credits roll and she's sleeping quietly next to me on the couch, the Christmas lights casting my living room in a calming glow augmented by the snoozing cats and flickering fire.

She joked about wanting it to be clear we're both claimed, like the rings will do the trick.

She has no idea.

CHAPTER TWENTY-THREE

Gruff

I arrive home on Friday to a house that smells like fresh pine and sugar cookies.

PB no longer ambushes me at the door, and RJ also seems to have accepted his new home, though he's still a bit of a recluse.

"Well, hey there, soldier," Andy says with a little twang in her voice as I reach the kitchen, though when I finally get a look at her face, she looks a bit perturbed.

"Everything okay?" I ask, because she's normally so sunny and bright when she greets me, I'm instantly curious about the expression.

She rolls her eyes and shakes her head before sliding a tray of cookies onto a metal rack. "I have an odd tendency to adopt a country-ish way of talking sometimes with you and I'm really not sure why." She laughs with a self-deprecating dip of her chin and shakes her head again.

"I hadn't noticed that in particular... only that it's nice to be welcomed home," I admit, then instantly feel foolish. I've said too much, but I can't deny I like her being here, especially now that I know to expect a cat at my feet, and she's not attacking me with flying books.

"Aw. I'm glad. I enjoy welcoming you home. I've had a great time with you this week." She beams, then focuses her attention on the cookies in front of her for a moment, holding the sheet in one hand and gently settling each cookie on the cooling rack.

"Me, too." I shift around, then grab PB and pick him up, cradling him like an infant. "I'm going to go change."

She flashes her brows. "Go ahead, baby, slip into something a little more comfortable." She winks and chuckles at herself, her focus back on the cookies.

I laugh, too, and I hope she can't tell it's forced. Because her calling me baby and using that slightly breathy voice, even in jest, has done something terrible to me.

Or maybe it's the last week of sharing dinners and watching movies on the couch after work. Maybe it's the tree she coaxed me into buying and decorating on Tuesday after she saw a guy selling them when she took the long way home.

We just sort of fell into the habit of sharing our lives and space on Monday and we've stuck with it. When she announced she wanted to get into the Christmas spirit tonight and watch Christmas movies and frost cookies, I happily agreed.

Maybe this should be some kind of warning to me, but I can't be bothered to second-guess this. Being around her feels different than anything I've had before.

It's easy with her... though the response to the guy in the coffee shop flirting with her and the subsequent barrage of self-recrimination for being so overt and aggressive wasn't. Sitting next to her on the couch and watching her laugh, coo at her cats, and just spread her joyous energy around has been no hardship.

The only difficult aspect to all of this has been this creeping sensation suggesting *maybe...*

She'll look at me while laughing and I'll join her because resisting is impossible and there it'll come... *maybe*.

I walk in the door, and she welcomes me home and the twinge in my chest whispers it—*maybe*.

I look at her while she's focusing on those little cookies, sliding each one painstakingly onto the cooling rack, and I want to toss *maybe* to the wind and round the counter and taste her.

I shut the door to my room and toss PB onto the bed. He gives me a crusty look and instantly hops down and swaggers over to the door, pressing one paw up on the wood to make his desires known.

"Got it, buddy. Give me a minute." I don't know why I want him in here, but I know I need a moment to change and maybe I want something of hers in here with me. I shuck my uniform top, then plunk down on the side of the bed to unlace my boots.

Will I miss this? There's a ritual in wearing a uniform and there's no way to expedite certain parts of it like combat boot laces being high maintenance. Will I miss holding a lighter to the loose threads on my OCPs or making sure my shoes are shined up when wearing any of the formal uniforms I don for military balls or visiting certain places?

Maybe? Maybe I will. I've certainly worn it with pride, but I also feel the longing for change. And I'm not really someone who *longs* for stuff. I live my life, do my work, and embrace reality.

Or, I used to be that way.

Lately, there's an influx of longing and it's not my favorite thing. I don't know how to manage those kinds of feelings.

A light knock on the door has PB scratching at the wood with all claws out and me rushing to open it.

"Hey, sorry to interrupt. Just wanted to see if you're still good with pizza for dinner? I'm super hungry so wanted to go ahead and order. I don't mean to rush you, though, so—"

She has her hair in a braid and the pink ends are hanging over one shoulder. And maybe it's because of the week we've had together and how like a vacation from real life it's felt when I walk in the door each evening, or maybe it's because she's so beautiful leaning in the doorway giving me that soft smile, but I don't resist the urge to reach up and tug ever so slightly on the end of her braid to halt her speech.

"It's fine. Pizza sounds good. Go ahead and order. I'll just be another minute." I drop her braid and step back. She nods quickly and shuts the door as she backs out, and I think I catch the slight tinge of a blush on her cheeks.

I sink down on to the bed again and finish removing my boots, then fall back on top of the blankets and press the heels of my hands into my eyes.

"What are you doing?" I ask the question out loud, but quiet enough she won't hear me, even if she's right outside.

I'm overthinking everything except how I act with her, and then I'm shooting from the hip, going with my gut, whatever else people say to show they are *not* overthinking. In fact, I'm barely thinking at all when it comes to her, other than about how much I like her and want to spend more time with her.

And this wouldn't be a problem, except it is. Because

this isn't about love or real marriage. This isn't about good feelings and fun. This is about getting her medical care and me convincing my family I'm not a basket case.

Apparently, despite all of my promises to myself, Andy, and every expectation I had when I suggested this plan, all of that is far easier said than done.

CHAPTER TWENTY-FOUR

Andy

We eat pizza on the couch. He has a lovely kitchen island and a nice six-person dinner table, but as the week has worn on and we've both been tired—him from long days at work and me from work and, I now know, my stupid failure of a parathyroid gland—we've resorted to eating with plates in our laps on the couch.

I never would've imagined doing this when I first arrived. But a little over two full weeks later, and I feel at home here. Or, almost at home. I don't feel like I can just walk into his room and start chatting, but in every other space, I'm good.

Though, when I do peek in on him and he does something like he just did where he pulled on my braid?

It makes me a little giddy.

And that's not helpful, is it? No. Because me and Wilson—Will—Gruff have an arrangement. I think we're building a friendship, too, much to my delight. Anything else is off the table.

But is it on the counter? The floor? The bed?

And there's the problem. My brain has decided to become a little saboteur. No longer does it allow me to enjoy Gruff's handsomeness objectively and appreciate his kindness and gentleness with my cats and simply conclude he's a better man than I ever imagined he could be when I met him last year. No.

It's much more than that.

This little brain has staged a coup against reason. Instead of accepting that I hardly know the man and that I'm here for the health insurance, it's latching onto small details I shouldn't notice.

It's lighting up at the way his crow's feet line the sides of his eyes when he smiles and makes my stomach swoop.

It's falling all over itself when he talks about his mom's accomplishments or how great his cousin is.

It's downright swooning when he's gentle with my cats, who've both decided he's not an evil overlord and have accepted him into their pack.

Brain, thou hast betrayed me.

Or something.

Because I can't unsee this version of him—the one with his stupidly attractive feet propped up on the table and his red, green, and gray flannel pants and a soft white T-shirt I desperately want to touch.

Ignoring the physical attraction between us would be simple. I did for a year, after all. But knowing he's a good man, he's hard-working but feeling a bit directionless and that freaks him out... these details make me *like* him.

More than like him.

They make me feel things for him I have no business

feeling for someone who has very clearly stated he's here for the equitable exchange of agreed upon outcomes—health insurance for me, and a wife-like person at his side over Christmas for him.

And yet... he's chuckling low as he pipes white frosting on a star-shaped cookie.

"I haven't decorated cookies since I was a kid, and it shows."

Never in a million years would I have anticipated this man being self-deprecating, and yet, here we are. I like it too much.

"It does take practice," I say, adding details to a Christmas tree. I flooded the background green and now I'm piping in strings of lights.

When I look up, he's scowling.

"You're very, very talented at this, Andy."

His intense tone has me curious. "Is that... bad?"

He huffs, a half-smile tugging at one side of his handsome face. "No. I just... I'm not sure I understand you. You're good at everything you do. Did you always want to own a café?"

I bluster, covering all manner of feelings with a too-loud laugh I'm certain he's smart enough to see through, but I can't go back. "No, not really. I've always loved interacting with people. I got a degree in design and tried working in the field for... a while. It didn't work out. I ended up working at Alex Brews about four years ago and I've been there ever since—though obviously, I'd planned to leave there and do my own thing before all the other stuff happened." The broken arm, the medical debt, the dream temporarily but absolutely deferred until I got my health and finances back on track. He knows all that. And still, this is more than I ever planned on telling him.

"Design. Interior?" He must have this on his mind after we talked about Janie.

"Graphic, actually. I worked for a design firm for a while but turns out it was not the dream job I'd hoped. I lasted as long as I could before abandoning ship." I'm leaving out a few things—my attempt to go freelance and build my own business, my deep depression after failing utterly to do so and deciding moving into a crap apartment and working at a cute coffee shop was better than the soul-killing work of my corporate job.

In my youth, I could be a bit black and white. It felt like all or nothing, and I went with nothing.

"I'm sorry design didn't work out, though I imagine you use the skill often." He nods at my cookie creation.

I laugh lightly, the old ache of failure not bothering me quite so much for some reason. "Yes, my cookie decorating skills are truly something to be adored. I also do the drawings on Alex Brews's windows so, you know, I'm getting my art out there."

He smiles, clearly recognizing this is far from what I'd dreamed for my design career, but kind enough not to point that out.

"I like the croissant with the Santa hat."

A giggle jumps out. "Silly as it is, those little talking pastries bring me an absurd amount of joy." And part of what I've loved about the cat café planning has been all the possibilities for cat-related design merchandise and advertising.

"It's not silly if it brings you joy. I'm realizing I need to identify what those things are for myself."

His serious gaze drifts down to his cookie and he jolts, then his eyes rise to meet mine and his horrified expression makes me laugh way too loudly.

"Well, things that bring you joy don't have to be pretty, right?"

His knitted brows relax, and then he grins—no—beams at me. This serious person who is a hard-working, determined man with salt and pepper hair and sexy fine lines breaks into a truly joyous laugh. I think Christmas carols are playing in the background, highlighting his smile and laughter which are a downright Christmas Miracle.

I want to make him laugh every day. Every single day for—well, for as long as I can.

My eyes are watering and I swipe at them, the laughter such a relief. He wipes at his cheek, then pulls his hand away and freezes.

"It's everywhere." He's looking at his fingers where there's white and red frosting merging into a garish pink. It's on his cheek, and I won't mention the bit I see on the sleeve of his shirt.

"Stay right there." I scuttle to the sink and get a rag, then position myself in front of him but away from the blast zone of his cookie decorating explosion. "Tilt your face down for me."

He does, gaze on me as I wipe at the curve of his cheekbone. It hasn't occurred to me until *right this second* how intimate this is. We're a few inches apart, and I'm smoothing a rag over his skin with one hand, the other gently cradling the other side of his face.

"Thank you," he says, his voice deliciously low and rumbly—so much so, I swear I can feel it in my chest.

"Of course." I bite my lip, trying to ignore the weight of his attention and wondering if the bags under my eyes are as obvious to him as they are to me. I'm not sleeping well, not resting fully, but that's one more thing that should improve with the surgery. One more reason I'm right here.

I pull away, then notice a little just to the side of his mouth. "One more little bit right here," I say, and then I'm looking at his lips.

I shouldn't have done it.

It's a huge mistake.

His cheek is fairly smooth but down here where a beard would go, he's got a little more than a five o'clock shadow after not shaving since this morning, at least, and it's making a bristly sound that is, for some reason, incredibly appealing.

Like, I want to kiss him so bad right now.

I want to feel the scrape of that stubble on my cheeks and chin and lips and—

A gasp slips out as I step back. "All set!"

I'm too cheery and weird, but I hope he doesn't notice. He can't know what was going on in my head, and I'm deeply thankful for that.

"Thanks for your help. And thanks for making the cookies and everything, even if I messed them up." He busies himself picking up a few sprinkles from the counter.

"There is no such thing as messing up Christmas cookies unless you swap the sugar with salt. Take a bite." I grab one of his cookies—they really do look like a total mess —and raise it for a toast. "To finding the joy in the mess and the beauty in the... well, the mess."

We chuckle at my lame toast, but he nods and touches his obscenely gory-looking cookie to mine.

"To enjoying the beautiful mess."

He takes a bite and I hold off, watching him. It is possible he doesn't like sugar cookies with frosting, and if so, then I've botched this whole thing. But we still bonded.

The light groan he lets out sends a thrill through me.

He chews avidly before saying, "You're right. It's ugly as all get out but tastes great."

I grin at him, more than a little pleased he's happy. "The best baked goods are always that way."

We finish our cookies, and he pops one more small one in his mouth before we clean up. We've had such a nice time this evening—the whole week. I'm not sure if it's because of or in spite of this that I ask, "Did you and your ex do stuff like this?"

He freezes for a moment, but jumpstarts into motion again fairly quickly, though his eyes stay on the countertop he's wiping. "Never."

Absorbing this, I move to sweep the floors, wishing I hadn't brought it up. He surprises me by offering more.

"She was... a hard person to love. I'm not sure that's even the right way to explain it, but she was never happy. If I thought things were going well, I was either ignorant or wrong. I don't actually remember a time when we did things just for the fun of it. There was always a purpose behind her choices in a calculated way."

"That sounds really difficult. But you must've gotten together for a reason."

It's more a question than a statement, and I'm not sure why I'm even asking it. Why do I want to know why he was with his ex when they are divorced?

His gaze climbs slowly up to meet mine. "I wanted to be what she needed. And I think she wanted to be what I did at first, too. But neither of us were good at being people we aren't." A smile flickers across his face, then dies out. He clears his throat and tosses the rag into the sink. "I'm going to get to bed. Have a good night."

He's gone in a matter of seconds, leaving me with the quiet living room and a low-burning fire. I thought we'd sip hot chocolate and have a few more cookies while we chatted or watched part of another movie, savoring the glow of the Christmas tree. Even on work nights, he stays up later than this.

My questions about his ex shut the door on more fun together. Not for the first time, I wondered if he's still broken-hearted. He certainly has some resentment toward his ex and marriage in general, at least in the past when he mentioned anything about it. But generally, he doesn't seem completely broken up about it... I think?

I snuggle up on his lovely cream couch with hot chocolate and two squishy cats and a heart brimming with questions about a man I should know better than to care this much for.

CHAPTER TWENTY-FIVE

Gruff

I haven't seen Andy for more than a few minutes in passing since Friday night.

She volunteered at a friend's business after work Saturday and Sunday, and though my unit has shifted to shorter days as the holiday and block leave period approach, she's been gone a lot. I don't think she's avoiding me—she's genuinely just busy living her life.

As she should be. She's not obligated to stay home and watch movies with me after work. I may have enjoyed it, but I'm not about to make it a condition of our agreement.

That'd be weird.

And sad.

Pathetic, actually.

It's bad enough that in three days, we'll be flying to Vermont, and she'll be meeting my family and getting a look at the whole mess in all its glory. We need to talk through details and figure out plans and probably hold hands once or twice so we don't look like it's our first time when we walk into the lodge with an audience, but I can't seem to bring that up when she waves at me as she slips out the door for her early shifts first thing in the morning, or when she tiptoes in late after... doing whatever she's up to.

I'm distracted enough by these thoughts and the looming duties of playing happy family man that I shut down my computer at only a little after three on the Wednesday before I start my holiday leave and put on a show for my family.

JJ appears in my doorway before I can sneak out.

"Slipping out before the rest of us, eh?" he asks, his general demeanor so much lighter since he met and married Grace.

"It's only you and me. Literally everyone else left hours ago."

He laughs softly. "I know. Just giving you crap."

"I know." I should laugh or summon a chuckle, but worry's nagging at me.

"What's going on?" He leans in the doorway and quite effectively blocks my exit.

"I'm grumpy."

He stares for a moment. "Shocking."

I grumble and exhale, then pace back to my desk and grab the fleece that matches my uniform from the back of my chair. It's chilly enough I'll be glad I have it, even if it's not dark yet.

"I'm seeing my family this weekend. Andy's going with me, and I feel like we need to settle some things, but it's..." I shake my head and sigh a bit dramatically. "It's a mess."

"Really?"

The skepticism in his tone has me eying him. "Yes."

He glares at me. "Man, I know. It's obviously a mess if you married a woman for a reason other than love. *Ask me how I know.*"

I roll my eyes. "I know. But you and Grace were different. Obviously."

He raises his brows and I miss when I was a jerk and he was my underling instead of my friend who stands up to me and doesn't take my crap.

"I just mean, it's different. I'm not going to fall in love with Andy, no matter how much I like her, and—"

The way his eyes narrow effectively change my tack.

"I'm saying we need to nail down the parameters of being a couple. I thought we'd go on a few more dates so we'd be comfortable, but time's up. And my mom's going to see straight through it. Everyone is."

He's still sort of squinting at me. "And it's important people don't see through your fake marriage because…"

I haven't explained this to him, but I'm not about to unpack that bag of antique garbage right now. "Not the point."

He shakes his head and steps backward into the hallway. "Fine. You'll tell me someday. But for now, my advice is to stop being an idiot and talk to your wife and be a team."

I glare at him, but he shrugs and trots off, leaving me to brood in my office for a few minutes before I finally do leave.

I'm annoyed with him because he's right. If I'm smart, I'll explain everything to Andy and we'll talk about what needs to happen openly, like adults who came into this with our eyes wide open.

When I walk in the door and PB greets me with a slide along my pant leg and flick of his tail, leaving a trail of cat hair behind, instead of reaching for the lint roller, I'm anxious to get the conversation over with.

Until Andy steps out of her room in a cocktail dress that, no lie, makes me want to beg.

I'm not even sure what I'd beg for, but this dress? It makes me want to do it.

Please.

"Oh, sorry. I was just trying on a few things because it sounds like your family is as fancy as expected based on the itinerary and I don't want to be out of place with my clothes." She mumbles something I don't catch, then pastes on a too-bright smile. "What do you think?"

I blink. Or maybe I don't. I can't be sure because my eyes are busy taking in the truly magnificent sight of her in this deep red dress. It's got a wide neck and shows a hint of her collar bones and shoulders, but long sleeves. It hits at the knee so I'm only privy to the smooth skin of her calves, but it's enough.

The rest of it hugs her curves in a way that short-circuits my brain. I know this because I can't recall what she just said, what she asked me, or what I'm supposed to do.

"Will? Are you okay? Is it another migraine?" She approaches in a few strides and gently reaches up to brush her fingertips across my forehead.

The contact rattles me out of the haze just like her words. *Will.* Immeasurably better than Gruff. I like my name on her lips so much it's stupid, but instead of sinking into the bliss of the sound, I summon focus for long enough to find words. "I'm sorry. No migraine. Just a weird day." Or, just me making this weird.

I've noticed Andy's beauty since the first time I saw her.

It's unmissable. And this dress doesn't show me anything I haven't been aware of... She's got curves in all the best places and she's strong and gorgeous. But she's normally in jeans for work or sweatpants for relaxing.

Seeing her dressed up like this has put me into an odd frame of mind.

"Good. Or, well, not good that it was weird, but I'm glad you're not hurting."

And there comes the compassion to ensnare me even more. "Me, too."

"I'll be out in a few," she says and turns to go. Her smile is more natural now as she heads toward the hallway, and the wide expanse of her back on display as she turns, the way the material hugs her so deliciously, finally pushes me to speak rather than choke on my tongue.

"Andy, the dress...."

She glances over her shoulder before she disappears down the hall.

"It's beautiful."

She flashes me a smile I can tell is truly pleased, and then she's gone.

I spend the next few minutes getting changed out of my uniform, arranging my bag and lunch for tomorrow so I don't have to think about it, and willing my pulse to calm. If she comes out in another dress, I might be in trouble.

But five minutes later, Andy wanders out holding RJ in one hand and her ereader in the other looking at ease as she slumps onto the couch. It's only now I realize she looks tired. Not just sleepy or like maybe she didn't sleep well the night before, but deeply exhausted.

"Are you feeling okay?" I'm tiptoeing into this conversation thanks to my past.

Andy is not my ex, but anytime I asked this question, it

was taken as an insult. If she looked tired, it was secretly a put-down. If she seemed like she might be overwhelmed and I asked how to help, it was me suggesting she couldn't handle anything on her own.

"Me? Yeah. I'm just worn out. I know we aren't going to Vermont to rest, but I feel like having a break from work and other stuff is much needed. I'm looking forward to it."

She releases RJ who scampers out of her arms and takes up residence on the back of the couch, a little black polka dot with his white belly tucked away on the bright red throw I got out in honor of the season.

I make a mental note to book Andy some time at the spa if that's not on the schedule yet. It won't take away all the exhaustion, but it could be good.

"You've been gone a lot. I was hoping it wasn't—" I don't like admitting how much I've wondered if she's staying away on purpose. I also don't like the idea of pretending any more than I already am. This may not be a real marriage based on love, but I like that it's clear. The agreement is clear, what we get is clear—or it will be soon— and lying now doesn't feel right. "That you were avoiding me."

She leans her head back on a pillow and watches me approach the couch with a bowl of popcorn and a water. I set them down, then return to the kitchen to grab myself a glass while she responds.

"I'm sorry. It's just been wild, and I'm feeling run down. I helped with En Mode Blanc's sample sale over the weekend, which was *way* more work than I anticipated but it was the least I could do after the owner let me borrow my wedding dress. Then we had the Alex Brews Christmas party, and then Grace and I got together and did our gift exchange last night. I had my appointment, which went well, and we got my surgery scheduled yesterday. And now, I'm here and I'm all yours, aside from work during the day, until we leave this weekend."

Her words hit me in a way they shouldn't and I can't think about anything other than those three words dancing in my mind, not even my questions about her surgery.

I'm all yours.

It's been so long since I wanted this from someone. In fact, I'm not sure I ever have. I thought I loved my ex, but I also thought I knew her. I never longed to have her or have *more* of her because... well, arrogantly, I thought I already did. By the time I had those future-facing feelings about marriage and a life together, we'd already enmeshed our lives enough that I thought it was all foregone conclusions.

With Andy, I have none of her. And going into this, I convinced myself I didn't want any of her except the façade of a wife when around my family.

In reality, I am facing the truth that I want more. More of her. More opportunity to see what we're like together.

I want her baking projects and brightly colored nails and flirting and cat obsession. I want her sprawled on my couch and, yes, in my bed.

I'd just like to be in there with her.

I clear my throat and set the glass on my coffee table and realize it has, yet again, been a little too long since she spoke and I responded, so I rush to fill the space. "Great. Good. I have work tomorrow and Friday but should be shorter days, and then we leave early Saturday."

She perks up. "Oh, good. Maybe we can talk over what you're packing and stuff at some point? I know clothing is not the most important thing here, but I'm also well aware that first impressions matter and you need your family to believe I'm the kind of woman you'd be with, so—"

"You *are* the kind of woman I'd be with," I say, sorry to interrupt her on principle, but in this moment, not so much.

She gives me a look I can't read.

"That's nice, but I think we both know that's not true. What did you say your ex-wife does for a living?" Her brows slowly raise to accentuate her point.

"She was involved with a non-profit. And now, she—"

Andy waves me off. "I don't think I even want to know. But my point stands. Your brother is some bigwig in the State Department, your father is a former senator, and your mother a prosecutor, and you're this impressive officer in the Army."

She swallows and I see the tension pulling at her mouth. She leaves the rest unsaid—she's a barista at a local coffee shop.

It's the way she slumps into the pillows that does it. I move quickly, sitting next to her on the couch and leaning over her so she's caged in by my arms as I pin her bright blue eyes with my gaze.

"You are a generous, empathetic, beautiful, thoughtful, intelligent, funny, resourceful woman who I am honored to have with me."

She blinks, lashes fluttering lightly, and her mouth drops open.

My attention falls to that full bottom lip that is without a doubt the most enticing color pink on the planet Earth, but I remember my purpose.

"I don't want you worried about them. I know I've made it seem like it's a tense situation, and it is. But who *you* are is irrelevant to the tension. It's old family dynamics and whether you are President or a general or princess or a barista who has absolutely no desire to do anything else other than pull espresso and make people's day with her warmth, that won't change. But *I'll* be better with you there."

Her endless blue eyes stay glued to mine and she whispers, "Okay."

An indulgent thought presses into my mind.

You should kiss her.

It's not as ludicrous as it should be, especially considering the way I keep falling into these moments and then climbing out with pickaxes and spiked shoes and the willpower that keeps me moving.

I'm aware of everything—her soft scent that's part coffee, part mint. Her hair streaming behind her on the pillow, and the way her mouth is *right. There.*

Her breathing changes, and I would swear on my life her pupils are getting wider.

It's PB, the quiet menace of the house, who interrupts the moment and saves me from doing something I can't come back from. He pops up between us, his collar clinking with the movement, and then he shimmies between us and takes up residence on Andy's chest.

Her gaze catches on mine for a half second before she grins down at her boy. "Staking your claim, huh, buddy?" She pets him gently, giving me a look that sends fire into my chest.

A look that says she knows how close I was to kissing her—to staking *my* claim.

I pull back, allllll the way back, and settle into my side of the couch. It's a real drawback to this gigantic sectional that we aren't forced to touch at all.

But it's for the best this way.

Probably.

Because I shouldn't be kissing my fake wife and confusing everything between us. It's a matter of time before we go our separate ways, and I don't have anything to offer her anyway.

So it's better this way.

Definitely.

Mothers Of Military Network Message board:

SCLDG: They're en route! Family Christmas reunion and the poor girl is about to be tossed into the fire.

JusticeLVR: Oh goodness. Be kind to her.

SCLDG: Of course I will! I have plans, but only for their benefit.

Vic: Always scheming.

CoolyKay: I can't wait to hear how it goes!

Vic: I'll live vicariously, so yes. Keep it coming.

JusticeLVR: Yes, absolutely. Grace and JJ are coming in two days so I'll be enjoying the fruits of my own labor soon ;)

Vic: We really should lay off. That said, I want you all to know C's mentioned getting assigned stateside next year. Maybe I'll get my own Christmas miracle.

SCLDG: Oh wonderful news! Hoping for the best for all of us.

Vic: Hear hear.

CoolyKay: Indeed!

JusticeLVR: Amen.

CHAPTER TWENTY-SIX

Andy

As someone who has barely been out of the state of Virginia, I have not flown often.

This is not my first flight ever, but it is my first one in first class.

I'm not going to lie. It is really nice. Very fancy and luxurious and I am sorry for the people who had to slowly march to the back of the plane to get crammed into the sardine cans that are the economy seats, but I am *so not sorry* to be sitting up here.

Gruff laughed at me when I marveled at the large seats and the free glass of champagne the flight attendant brought me. It was a charmed laugh, not a mean-spirited one. He's had this fond look on his face all day, but when the captain announces we're starting our initial descent, I notice a shift.

He's stiff. Shoulders. Neck. Jaw tight. Posture unnaturally straight, which isn't entirely unusual for him when I see him in uniform but not normal sitting in this cushy seat.

"So... last call for prep time. What don't I know that I should?" I've asked this at least once before, and I don't want to seem like I'm pestering him, but I still don't know what the vaguely mentioned family drama is.

Maybe I really don't need to know.

But it feels like I probably should.

Y'know. As his wife and all.

His brow is so furrowed, it should be a before photo for Botox. And I'm not saying the man needs anything, but I have clearly hit a nerve and now he is showing me the truth in his broody expression.

"Janie is severely allergic to almonds."

A sharp "Ha!" erupts from me, and I clap a hand over my mouth. Not appropriate here in the sophisticated realms of first class, but also a weird response to him telling me about his cousin's food allergy.

It's just so far from what I expected him to say.

"Death by anaphylaxis is comedy gold to you?" he asks.

Even this has me smiling. He's stone cold serious but the words... the words *feel* like he's teasing me.

"Absolutely not. My mom is allergic to shellfish and I take all allergies seriously at work and otherwise. I genuinely have no idea why you presented that as if it's need to know, though." I'm smiling at him and he narrows his eyes.

"You might give her a pastry. Better not be almond cream-filled."

I rest my head back and a breathy chuckle sneaks out. "You are weird."

When I glance at him, he's eying me and has the tiniest little smile on his face. "You are, too."

I shrug. "You're not wrong."

My ears pop and despite my inexperience, I know this means our clock is ticking. "So, really. Help me feel like I'm not walking into this thing blindfolded."

He shifts around, his big body making the spacious seat seem small, and he looses a sigh. "It's not pretty. I guess that's why I haven't wanted to get into this. You're about to see all the pettiness and jealousy and nasty things that've been stored away. I try not to think about it, but it's going to be up in our faces all week." He finishes his ice water and hands the plastic cup to the flight attendant, who also swipes my empty cup from my hand.

"I'm not proud of who I become around them—my brother especially." His jaw flexes and I wonder what that means.

Who does he become?

Is he more like the person I assumed he was—taciturn, selfish, and brusque? Or is it some other version of Wilson Gruff I haven't seen?

"I'm sorry this is going to be so hard on you," I say, genuinely hoping all of his worries are for nothing.

My family never had much drama. We just aren't close. My parents never seemed to love having a kid so when time came for me to move out, I never looked back. They love me in the way they can, but they mostly live their lives. It's fine.

It's one thing about this situation I'm diving headfirst into that throws me for a loop—if being with his family is so awful, why go? Why not just beg off until, eventually, the distance is enough that there's no need for an excuse. That's where I am with my folks, and I think they prefer it. There's no bad blood, just time and years spent apart so that now, they live their lives and I live mine, and we catch up via text and phone calls on birthdays.

Maybe it's sad, but it's okay with me. And it isn't this—something that seems like it might be causing Gruff genuine pain.

He heaves another sigh. "It'll mean a lot to my mom. And it won't be all bad. I haven't been in years but this place we're staying is beautiful. We'll have some fun."

I looked at the resort website for approximately five hours total over the course of this week after he gave me the name, so I know he's telling the truth on that note.

It's gorgeous, and even if it's a little early for full snow coverage, they make snow and do all kinds of things to make sure it's a winter wonderland.

Northern Virginia is hit or miss on snow and rarely has much for long, so I'm all for a wintry escape, especially if it's with him.

I jolt a little in surprise at that thought, but he doesn't notice since there's a little bump of turbulence at the same time.

As a fairly sunny person, I wouldn't normally stress too much about a trip like this. It's one of my superpowers. But I'm ready to admit I'm more than looking forward to this trip. If it weren't for the giant question mark surrounding the family drama and whatever my job will be to make it not terrible for him, I'd be downright excited.

The truth is, I like him. We've hardly seen each other this week and I've missed him. Those aren't helpful thoughts, but they're true.

Another swoop sends our heads bobbing as the plane continues its downward path and his head falls back against the head rest. He turns toward me, and those gray-blue eyes are, startlingly, a little lost.

My heart squeezes.

He's such a direct, certain person. I hope I can do what

I need to. I hope I don't let him down. I hope what I do is enough to make him feel like all of this marriage and living together was worth it for him.

Shoving away those selfish thoughts, I enter go mode on the Good Wife Project. I reach for his hand where it's resting on his side of the pleasantly wide armrest and lace our fingers together. Nerves flip flop in my belly, and I set a hand on his arm. "I'm on your team. Whatever happens, I hope you know that."

CHAPTER TWENTY-SEVEN

Gruff

My parents wait inside the lobby like they own the resort.

Their friends do, so maybe they aren't entirely off in their very comfortable position of welcoming us through the doors of the picturesque wood and stone structure that looks like every wintry dream a person could imagine. The only resorts I've been to that surpass the cozy and luxurious combination of Maple Mountain are out West in the Rockies.

"Wilson," my father says, extending his hand. He's wearing chinos and a plaid button-down with a navy sweater overtop. Dressed down as far as he goes save bedtime and swimming pools, I imagine.

"Dad." One up, one down, and done. Always the same. As a politician, he always knew how to get the job down and then exit the scene. He won't mention any of the things I'm worried about—not yet.

"So glad you could come," my mother says, drawing me into a hug, but then jumping back. "Oh my goodness, forgive me. Andy, honey, welcome to the family."

She practically shoves me away and is now embracing Andy, who doesn't seem bothered by the hug so much as surprised. If she was expecting coldness from my parents, that's not what she'll get.

My mother's sporting a deep red pantsuit that should be jarring but seems at once comfortable and stylish with a side of seasonal. She's got a little Christmas wreath brooch pinned on one lapel where a US flag used to sit. As usual, she's fully herself with her silver hair pulled neatly away from her face and moderate makeup giving her a polished air.

"Yes, yes. Glad you could come. I'm Wilson Gruff, Senior." My father extends his hand to her, and inserts the warm addition of a hand cupping the back of Andy's when she shakes. Just the once up and down, though, naturally.

"Thank you so much. I'm happy to be here." She leans toward me, her shoulder knocking gently into my arm as she looks up at me. "Very happy."

Despite the stress that has been systematically wending its way through me with each mile we've traveled toward this reunion, Andy's bright blue eyes and the slight blush on her cheeks make me buy exactly what she's selling.

If I didn't know better, I'd think she really was completely happy to be here meeting my family.

"Wonderful. Well, your room keys are here." My mother hands Andy a little envelope full of what must be keys and likely a resort map. "Wilson, get the—" She flaps her hand in a gesture only a husband could interpret, and my father moves swiftly to pick up a basket full of goods. He hands it to me.

"These are a few little welcome gifts to help make sure you're comfortable. Janie and Chip arrive later, as does your brother." Her smile is perfect, practiced, and betrays no anxiety over the inevitable meeting ahead. She's dealt with it in her own mind and must expect I have, too.

I hope I have.

"Thank you so much. This is amazing," Andy says, reaching for her bag, then looking around with a start because it's already gone.

"Oh, don't worry. The bellman already got them and they're on the way to your room." My mom winks at Andy, who chuckles.

"Oh, good. It wasn't an early Grinch attack."

My mom grins and my dad laughs a little too loudly. Andy's eyes find mine and we share a look that I think means my folks are over the top, but I'm not sure. I don't know if I have that connection with her yet... or at all. I've gotten to know her fairly well over the last few weeks of living together, but I know there's so much left to learn.

I thank my mom and dad and we head to the elevators. I'm anxious to find our room and take a breath. Maybe we'll walk around the resort and explore a little. I want to stay busy until we get past the first meeting. Then it'll be fine. Everyone can deal with things and we'll all move on.

It'll be fine.

"Well, your parents are nothing like I thought they'd be like." She's leaning a shoulder against the elevator as it ascends.

"They're not bad. I'm sorry if I gave you the wrong

impression." They're wonderful, really. At least my mom is. My dad puts on a good show for me, but when we see Jason later, I'll be reminded yet again how much closer he is with my brother.

At forty-two, I really shouldn't feel that so keenly. I'm not sure I would if things were different.

"No, no. I made assumptions. I knew your dad was a senator and recently retired. I built up this idea of your mom and it wasn't like that at all." Her eyes are wide and she grips the thick braid of hair falling over her shoulder.

I want to do the same.

I have yet to touch her hair beyond that one little tug at the ends, and it is a thing I think about. Not in a creepy way, but just in a, *wouldn't it be nice* kind of way.

"Don't worry about it. They can be intense. But they're not bad." The doors open and we exit, entering an opulent hallway with ornate carpeting in red, brown, and blue tones. Every hallway sconce has a Christmas ribbon tied on.

This feels excessive, but who am I to say? Some people like ribbons, I guess.

We arrive at the door and Andy swipes the key. We enter to find a lavish sitting room with a loveseat, chair, fireplace, and desk to one side. There's a flat screen television and a wet bar with a small sink and countertop, coffee maker, and a larger-than-average mini fridge next to it. The bathroom door appears to be around the corner, and beyond the sitting area is a king-sized bed with crisp white linens and a red and green flannel-looking throw.

Just the one bed.

And silly me, I'd figured I'd sleep on the couch if needed.

"This room is gorgeous," Andy says, sliding into the space and dropping her purse into one of the sitting chairs.

She runs a hand along the marbled fireplace and grins as she takes it all in.

I see the moment she registers the bed. Her energy skips —almost freezes.

"Yeah. Because we're married." I say this out loud like we're sharing the same thought. Maybe we are.

"Of course. I don't know how I didn't think of it." She bites her lip and slowly approaches the bed. Her fingers trail along the bright white comforter.

My pulse is climbing with every inch she walks, and I spit out, "I'll request a rollaway," right as she says, "It's plenty big for the both of us."

We both halt then, and she slowly raises her eyes to mine. Then she bursts out laughing.

"You're going to get a rollaway?"

"Of course. It'll be fine."

Her head tips to the side. "And you don't think that'll seem strange to anyone? What if your mom comes to the door? One step inside and she'll see it."

Damn. I hadn't thought of anyone visiting us but knowing my mother, she'll want to check in. I wouldn't put it past her.

I sigh and scrub a hand over my face. Andy didn't bargain for this, and I didn't either, frankly, though it'll cause us pain in different ways, I suspect.

Her hand removes mine from my brow and she's close, earnest eyes gazing up into mine. "I feel fine about us sharing."

I swallow hard.

"You're not going to do anything to make me uncomfortable. I know that." Then she brushes a hand along my cheek and it's all I can do not to lean into it, press her palm more fully against my face. "I trust you."

With a nod, I accept her offer.

She trusts me.

I am grateful. Honored.

And desperately hoping that by the time we come back to this bed, after she's met everyone, seen everything, she'll still feel the same.

CHAPTER TWENTY-EIGHT

Andy

G ruff is pacing the room when I exit the bathroom after refreshing my makeup and tidying up my hair in preparation for the cocktail hour.

I'm not in a dress because our printed schedule included in the gift basket indicated *casual dress*. I suspect casual might mean different things, but when Gruff insisted I wear jeans, and promised me he was going to, I agreed.

Wearing comfortable, familiar clothes wouldn't be all bad. Plus, his parents had already seen me in my travel clothes which were cozy joggers, sneakers, and a large sweatshirt. I'd already failed the glam traveler look, but since there are designer sweatpants these days, I'm not spending another second worrying about that.

I will, however, take a moment to pep talk myself in the mirror before I dive into the Gruff family reunion.

"You may be a barista and wanna-be cat café owner in

the midst of former senators, lawyers, and other incredibly impressive people, but you are still a valuable human being. You are kind and funny and Gruff is the one who started all of this so if he's not happy with how this goes, it's really his fault anyway." I make an exaggerated cheesy smile, then wink at myself.

I kept the makeup light, but it still looks good. My hair is cooperating beautifully thus far, especially considering it was drizzling when we left home this morning. It's still in the braid, but I haven't sprouted wings at the sides of my head due to humidity, so it still looks purposeful and not like I couldn't decide between a ponytail and actually styling my hair and resorted instead to a braid.

I eye the cream-colored sweater. It's insanely soft and feels fancy thanks to how it drapes over one shoulder. It's a small travesty I'm wearing a strapless bra, but this look dresses up the sweater and may compensate for my jeans if I end up feeling too casual thanks to those. And the jeans are fine. I topped it all off with cute bright red loafer-style slip-ons, my level-up from sneaks.

I'm self-conscious as I approach him where he's pacing, eyes on the window that shows a view of the ski resort's base.

"Sorry that took a minute. I'm all set." My voice is froggy, betraying my nerves, but I'm not going to give in to them. I can do this.

We can do this.

He turns and his eyes take me in—face, sliding down my braid, a jump to the bare shoulder and my décolletage, then a quick slip town to jeans, shoes, and back up.

He swallows hard.

"You're beautiful." It's all he says for a moment, his

intense gaze stirring up those nerves I've just promised myself I won't be defeated by.

"Thank you. I like your sweater." It's a Fair Isle-style thing with navy, burgundy, red, and white. It should be almost too much, but the pattern is subtle enough to just look sophisticated and a little cheery.

"Thanks. My mother's handiwork a few years back. I make a point to wear it every year." His slight smile makes me grin.

"Smart man."

He nods, then holds out a hand toward the door. I head that way, wondering if I need a purse or at least an ID or maybe my ereader so I can sneak in some reading time if they're all chatting and I'm left to myself.

No. No, we will not be sneaking away. This is the whole reason we're married!

We're quiet in the elevator until right before the doors swing open, when he turns to me with urgency.

"I appreciate you doing this. And I'm sorry."

The doors roll open and despite what fantasy nightmare scenarios I've dreamed up, there's no big crowd of people holding champagne glasses in formal wear to greet us. I'm instantly at ease.

But Gruff is not. He's rigid and stern and all the things I know he becomes when he's stressed out. I like that I know this, and I'm going to help him.

"Come on, husband," I say, and grab his hand, threading our fingers and tugging him toward the area I am fairly certain we're supposed to be meeting his family in. This feels like a momentous thing, holding hands, and yet I'm acting like it's no big thang because we're married and of course we do this all the time. Thankfully, no one can see how my stomach flips every time we touch in any way.

His eyes are on me but he says nothing. I wonder if he has social anxiety? Or if this really is about his family.

"Willy!"

A voice rings out and then someone rushes toward us. She's a gorgeous brunette with long straight hair and golden skin and she looks the kind of effortlessly glamorous I will never achieve.

She launches into Gruff's arms and he chuckles and hugs her with his free hand. I drop the one I'm holding and he completes the embrace for a moment before they both pull back.

The woman's face is honestly kind of tragic. How does someone this beautiful exist in real life? I can't help but feel a little sad for her because, if this is her actual face and not a mirage, then she has never had to struggle.

Okay, fine. That's dramatic, but truly. She's stunning. Stun. Ning.

"Janie, this is my wife, Andy." Gruff slips his arm around my shoulders and pulls me close. "Andy, this is my cousin, Janie."

Ah, the cousin! "I've been looking forward to meeting you! You're so talented." If she really did decorate his apartment, then *wow*. She's got the beauty and the brains.

Honestly, how rude, right? Like, how does one person luck out with all of that in one ridiculously fit and stylish package?

Janie's grin is wide and delightful. "I am so dang happy to meet you!" She pulls me into her arms and gives me a truly world-class hug.

When she releases me, she steps back and beams at me and Gruff.

"You guys are adorable. We've got Tall, Dark, and

Moody over here and Little Miss Sunshine on his arm. How's it working out?"

Gruff mentioned on the plane that Janie knew our secret, but so far she's not being too overt about it.

There's a sparkle in her eye that feels like a hint, though. I glance up at Gruff to see him glaring at her.

"Janie." It's a warning.

Her lips pinch but she fails to hide her smile. "Willy."

I chuckle.

He pins me with a look. "Don't get any ideas."

Janie's laugh echoes around the room and all heads turn toward us. I'm relieved it's not because of me, but the spotlight hits us anyway. Janie waves them away and turns her back on the crowd, and I do my best not to crane my neck to see who's already here. There are at least twenty people so that's... well, a lot more people than I expected.

"Don't worry about all of them," she says, tossing a look over her shoulder. "And no, they're not here yet."

Gruff nods tightly. "Fine."

Janie's joyful, playful demeanor shrinks a touch. "It'll be fine."

I loop Gruff's arm in mine. "It will be."

His quick glance at me, then back to Janie feels... pointed. I'm about to question this vibe when a dull roar rises up. That sounds fantastical, but it's no lie. There's literally an uptick in conversation and someone starts clapping, and it's then I see everyone's attention is pinned behind me and Gruff.

Janie's expression is the second clue—she shifts into something guarded, closed. It's so different from everything I've seen from her in the last few seconds, I doubt I'd recognize her if I met her like this.

But as we turn, it feels like we're moving in slow motion.

My arm looped in Gruff's, the air thick with apprehension, I set eyes on two people walking up to the lounge area. They are vaguely matching like stylish couples in movies do with touches of the same color schemes—black, red, gold and hints of similar style, even though he's wearing black slacks and a button down layered with a gray sweater with red accents over top, and she's wearing a fitted red Christmas sweater I'd bet money is cashmere. It clings to her petite frame and accentuates her prominent baby bump.

Oh. Ohhhh. I wonder if this is part of the angst? If an imminent child is what makes this so awkward, and if Gruff had come as a single man it would seem he's that much farther from the same place in life?

Maybe. It doesn't quite click. There's some level of competition and comparison between the brothers—I've gathered this much.

The couple is lit from above by what looks like spotlights but is actually conveniently placed recessed lighting in the ceiling as they approach the bar. They can't walk into the party and greet the parents until they get past us, so I'm internally bracing for this first meeting.

"Ah, Willy. It's been so long." The man, who absolutely looks like a younger, slightly less handsome version of his brother, moves all the way into our space, and I slip my arm out of Gruff's just in time to avoid being wrapped up in a hug.

Huh.

"It has," Gruff says, his voice graveled.

They separate and Gruff is stiff as a board. I mean, I'm not sure I've seen him so completely closed in on himself with tight lips, his whole being bronzed into a statue's version of a human body.

"This is my wife, Andy," he says, his hand finding the small of my back.

You're up!

A broad smile paints my face as I say, "It's nice to meet you. Both," I say, because I look toward his brother's wife and give Gruff a look as though to say, "shouldn't you introduce me to your sister-in-law?"

"Andy, this is my brother, Jason, and Elaine." He clears his throat but doesn't say anything else.

Elaine seems a little uncomfortable, too, but she takes my hand once Jason has released it.

"Nice to meet you, Andy. And good luck." Her eyes flare and Gruff's brother mumbles something about seeing their parents, but I'm too busy watching Gruff, Janie, and another man who must be their cousin Chip.

They look like they've walked through a mine field. And I'm more certain than ever I'm missing something.

Gruff

First meeting over.

Andy handled herself well. Though I expected no less.

I am counting the minutes until it's appropriate to leave. They've passed four kinds of appetizers. We've gone through meeting my aunts and uncles, the friends my parents invited, and I introduced Andy to the only other ally here, Chip. Thank Christmas my cousins are here because being alone with these people would be unbearable.

I've got guilt piling up on me at the same time I refuse to clue in Andy. I just can't bring myself to do it, especially not when I see her laughing with Janie and genuinely seeming to have a great time. Across the room, my brother and Elaine are chatting with the Gorsons and they are nice enough people but I can't stand the way my brother is glad-handing at what is supposed to be a family event.

Granted, when the *family* turns into this mishmash of people we are actually related to and people he wanted my parents to invite in order to impress them, I'm not sure we can really call this a family gathering.

Oh, well.

"Are you okay?"

It's Janie's voice, familiar and kind, that pulls me from my brooding. Which, by the way, I hate that I'm doing. I wish I could be chatting with people I've known most of my life or even catching up with Chip. But he seems to recognize I'm not in the mood to talk, and Janie kept Andy occupied once we made our rounds and did all the introductions.

"I'm fine." It's unconvincing, but what am I supposed to say?

"You know, I'm worried about Andy."

This has my head snapping toward her. "What? Why? What happened?"

Her lovely face lights up with a soft smile. "I knew it."

My eyes narrow on her. "You know what?"

"You like her."

I mumble something unintelligible that even I'm not sure is something she should be able to understand.

"You do. Oh... you *more* than like her." She's got a Cheshire cat grin like this is the best news.

"Hush, you little pest. That's irrelevant." I duck so I'm closer to her ear and my eyes skate around to make sure no one is listening. "No one else knows."

Janie, who is the only person who knows my marriage is a sham because she's the only person willing to call me out on why I didn't invite anyone to the wedding and certainly the only person I admitted the truth to, rolls her eyes.

"Oh, really? I had no idea."

The sass in her tone should grate, but it only makes me roll my eyes right back at her like we're still kids. I may be a decade older than her, but we were close growing up and we've stayed friends as adults.

"But seriously. She is adorable and so funny and I..." She drops her voice and keeps her head angled toward me while she speaks even though she's looking over at my brother. "I'm worried you haven't told her the truth."

My jaw locks tight and I exhale, trying to remind myself that in a matter of minutes, I can justifiably leave this place and escape to my room for at least twelve hours before anyone will expect to see me again.

"I will."

She turns her full attention to me. "You need to. Just get it over with and maybe you can actually relax and have fun."

Her compassion and genuine care for me are evident. I know she's right.

"I will."

"You will, what?" Andy asks, smiling up at me with one of the signature cocktails of the evening—the cranberry crush—in hand.

"I was just promising Janie I'll loosen up a bit. Have fun while we're here."

Andy's face brightens and she grins at Janie, then me. "I hope so. Can we go tubing?"

The hope in her voice and the way her eyebrows pinch to accentuate her anticipation does something to my insides.

"Of course. Let's do it tomorrow."

Janie smiles brightly and looks at her watch. "I'd love to

join you guys, but we've got family ski time tomorrow." Her eyes widen but she cracks and smiles again. "I think you're good to go, should you find yourself wanting to—"

"Say no more. I agree." I slip a hand down to Andy's waist, reveling in the feel of her soft sweater against her body. "Let's go get some real food."

Andy happily strolls with me, though she insists on making our excuses to my mother. While I appreciate the thought, I think my mother would understand us leaving after more than an hour doing the socially acceptable rounds.

Even so, I like how Andy wants to make sure to check in with my parents and tell Chip it was nice to meet him. She doesn't bother with anyone else specifically, though ends up sending farewells and friendly little waves and smiles to a few others on her way out.

She's just so damn likeable. Anyone who talked to her tonight isn't wondering what she does for a living, they're wondering how I managed to convince her to marry me.

Bribe her with above-average health insurance and a decent living situation.

The thought is more than a little depressing, but I refuse to get bogged down in it as Andy and I approach the brasserie located in another section of the resort.

"Everyone seemed really nice," she says as we settle into a small, polished wood booth.

I nod, not wanting to dump all my baggage at her feet and make the next few days harder. "They are. Good people, for the most part."

One eyebrow raises at me. "Hmm. Loaded. But let's get some food in us before we dive into the hot goss because I've had two cranberry crushes on an empty stomach and I don't need that kind of truth serum right now."

She hasn't seemed even remotely tipsy, but when she catches my eye and gives me a wink, I think maybe I can see she's a little soft around the edges. I wouldn't mind knowing what she really thinks of me and, if she's feeling loose, maybe it's a good opportunity to simply ask. Of course there's a line here, and I have no intention of crossing it by asking anything too personal. But I do want to see if she might give me... more.

"If you have something to say, I'm happy to hear the unfiltered version." I am more than a little curious, but the waiter approaches, and we both order before she responds.

She drops her elbows to the table and squints over at me like she's evaluating me for some kind of mission.

"Your dad is still very much a politician. And your mom is awesome. And your brother and his wife are..."

Of course she trickles off at this part, and it's all I can do not to prompt her. *What? What are they?*

It's immature and I'm not proud of it, but some part of me feels like how she views my brother is deeply important.

Like maybe my future with her, *our* future, hinges on her assessment of my brother before the events in our past boils over and she can't unknow things.

"I don't know. They seem a little fake, but I also don't want to be a jerk and I know I tend to have an internal bias against really beautiful people."

"Really?" I ask, because this turn has taken me a little aback.

"Yes. I mean, look at them. He's like a slightly less hot version of you and she is... I mean, good grief. She is stunning. The only woman in the room who outshines her is Janie. And oh my gosh!" She slaps the table and gives me a wide-eyed stare. Before I can fully appreciate that she has just called me hot, she continues, "Can we talk about how absolutely gorgeous your beautiful fairy princess angel goddess unicorn mermaid of a cousin is?"

I make no attempt to stifle my laugh because this woman is ridiculous. And also problematically appealing right now. "Don't let her hear you say that."

Andy's brows drop low. "That she's a fairy princess angel goddess unicorn mermaid? I feel like that's fairly high praise."

I laugh loudly enough that our waiter arrives at the table with a grin on his face as he delivers drinks and a big basket of fries. "You two are fun."

"We so are," Andy says, then winks at me.

My heart, the one that has felt a little shriveled all night, squeezes in a pleasure-pain sort of way I don't know what to do with. I don't know that anyone has ever called me *fun*, and I haven't ever felt it. I'm suddenly wondering how much fun I've actually experienced in my life before Andy became a part of it.

The waiter leaves us, promising we'll have our burgers in just a few minutes, and when he leaves, Andy grabs a fry and takes a big bite, then eyes the remaining portion with something like suspicion.

"I know this whole trip is tense for you, but I have to say, I'm having a great time. I mean, these fries... like who brings fries for the table instead of chips or bread? But here they are, dropping a basket of perfectly salted, crisp fries right in front of me like a dream."

I chuckle, savoring the lightness pervading my body despite the context. "All the food here is excellent. I say eat anything and everything that sounds good while we're here —you won't be disappointed."

She extends a hand with the most serious expression I've seen her wear. "I accept this challenge."

This draws another grin. Instead of shaking and releasing, I keep hold of her hand and lower mine down to the table. She follows suit, so now we're hand in hand across the table.

"Thank you for being here. And for being so charming. You really won everyone over."

Her smile is soft when she responds. "I'm glad I'm here. And I know I'm only partly getting a feel for things, but it seems like it's going pretty well."

I swallow and she instantly zeroes in on it.

"But not that well?" She sighs and pulls away, selecting another fry and shoving it in her mouth.

I can tell she wants to say something else, but she's literally just shoved multiple fries in her mouth to keep from saying anything.

"It is going well," I rush to reassure her. "It's just messy." And I haven't explained why.

I will. But for now, I work to distract her. "Don't worry about that, though. Let's talk more about how my brother is the less hot version of me?"

CHAPTER THIRTY

Andy

I have stuffed myself with the best burger I've eaten in recent memory and I'm walking through the most gorgeous resort I've ever seen with the sexiest man I've ever known in real life and, well, life is good.

Though I do have the sense I'm living under a gossamer veil of blissful ignorance that could be torn away any moment, I'm not questioning it. Gruff has no reason to keep me out of the loop unless it's for a purpose. So I'm going with the flow.

"Thanks for walking with me. I don't think I can go to bed this full," I say, trying not to swoon when I take in his handsome profile.

It's silly, but Vermont really does something for him. Or maybe it's the laughter we shared over dinner and his ribbing me about my slip calling him hot. He's been nice and relaxed around me, but he hasn't been playful like that before and it's really... it's really getting me.

I have this energy buzzing through me I need to channel somewhere. It's probably an extrovert's post-event high or something, but I know for a fact I'm hours away from sleep despite the exhaustion that should be setting in after a long day of travel, adjusting to a new place, navigating whatever unseen landmines are around me, and meeting a billion people wanting to know when we got married and why they weren't invited.

Happily, they all accepted that it was Gruff's second marriage, and that I never wanted a big to do easily enough. Or maybe they know Wilson Gruff, Junior well enough to know he wouldn't want anything splashy.

But now? I want adventure. A little more fun before bed that has nothing to do with the family drama I'm blind to or the agenda already set for our time here.

"Will you go on a quick side trip with me?" I ask, squeezing his hand a little for emphasis.

We're walking hand in hand because it feels natural to do so as husband and wife and we want to make sure this looks real to anyone casually observing.

I also do not mind this because he has great big, warm hands that make me feel good just holding onto them.

"This feels loaded, but sure. Why not?" he says, his eyes smiling at me.

"Alright. Come on." I tug him after me down the hallway, around the corner, and then out into a crystalline night. The moon is beaming down on us where we stand and the mountain range is arched in perfect spread like a card shark's hand. Behind us, there are white twinkle lights wrapped around the trees nearest the building and strung along the gutters and eaves of the resort itself.

We both suck in air because it is cold. Like, well below freezing.

"Crap, I didn't realize it would be this cold," I say, reluctantly dropping his hand and wrapping my arms around myself.

"Vermont in December after dark has a tendency to be rather wintry."

I give him an unimpressed look because as snarky as this man can be, sometimes his sass cracks me up, and I refuse to let him see it.

"Come on. We're on a mission."

He follows me off the patio, and I slip and slide a bit as we traverse an icy walkway.

"This feels ill-advised."

I turn to look at him, swinging my whole body around because I've tucked myself into as much of a little shell as possible and don't dare stretch my neck to see him and risk more exposure to my skin.

Why did I think going outside without a jacket was smart?

"Almost there." We arrive at the base of the resort where skiers can ski all the way up to the patio before returning to booted reality. The snow is thin down here, not surprisingly for December, but there's a fluffy layer on top.

I reach for him again. "Be bold with me, Will." A thrill of energy at calling him by the name no one else seems to use races through me.

Something flashes in his eyes and he steps forward. My stomach flips and I briefly consider staying here and seeing if he'll continue his progress all the way to me, but instead I sit, then lay down.

"What are you doing?"

I laugh and maybe also wheeze from the cold. "Snow angels. Come on. Do it with me."

He scowls and stands there with his hands on his hips, watching me flail around in two inches of snow, and I'm certain he's going to march away or just keep watching and let me continue my madness solo.

But he doesn't.

He grunts as he lowers himself to the frozen ground, then lays back.

"Now angel it, soldier. Spread your wings and flare your little angel robe out with your feet," I order.

I can see the cloud of hot air escape him as he sighs, but he does it, snow-angeling like a pro.

"Very good. Excellent work." I can't help but laugh with a joy that makes me feel like I might be borderline giddy at the way he's done this with me.

Andy of a year ago would never believe Colonel Gruff would do a thing like this. Not in a million years.

Would he have? Is this what he's like with everyone? Or, maybe, is this version of him one only I get to see?

I keep moving my arms, mostly because I think if I stop, I'll realize just how cold it is and we'll have to go in, but I notice he's halted, his attention on the sky.

"Sometimes, I forget what a difference it makes."

"What makes?" I ask, not sure I'm following.

"The ambient light. Up here, you can see so much more." His attention hasn't left the truly magnificent view of the sky when he says, "It's breathtaking."

I don't know why I like this word choice so much—maybe because the cold is beginning to actually steal my breath—but I do. I like how he's not afraid to say things like this to me, even if they only eke out a little at a time.

"It is. It's so big out there. I like feeling like a small part of this wild, expanding universe."

He hums softly. "A good reminder."

I want to ask him what it's a reminder for, but the wet layer of new snow has melted beneath me and I'm feeling the chill in a more substantial way. And by that, I mean my butt is completely numb, my hands are achingly cold, and my mouth feels sluggish from the chill. Best guess is I'm wet from head to heel.

"Okay, I think we're good." I sit up, then start to stand, but my feet slip.

Gruff is already on his feet—spry for a man his age, though I don't make the joke since I'm currently glued to the ground—and he reaches for me.

He pulls me up, up, up, and in a world-spinning move, I'm plastered against him, one of his hands at my lower back and the other still holding mine. We're close enough that we're inches away, and without the layers of appropriate clothing we absolutely should be wearing, I am basically spread over him like butter on toast.

"Okay?" he asks, his breath a warm whisper between us.

He smells really good. Clean and masculine, plus that chilly snow smell all around us. It's intoxicating. The air between us shimmers with possibility, and it's almost like this wintry night knows this is the closest we've ever been. It's as though the moon set us up and now the stars are waiting to see what's next.

"Yeah. Good. Just c-cold."

His arms tighten around me, but then he turns and he's guiding us back inside. The moment is lost—sorry, stars, we missed the cue.

It's only as we get into the elevator that I realize just

how cold my hands are. They're starting to ache now that they're warming up.

His big hands cup mine. They are fractionally warmer than mine.

"S-sorry. That was s-stupid." I look up to find him giving me one of those looks that makes my stomach swoop.

"I had fun." His eyes track between mine and he steps closer.

My pulse rockets into my throat and I am about to shout *yes! kiss me!* when the elevator doors slink open. He startles and steps out, guiding me forward and not releasing my hands.

I don't know why my heart is begging to be crushed, but it is.

It's nothing completely new for me, but these moments between us are cropping up more often. I can't imagine he's on the same page with all his preoccupation with family, and pretending, and his past. And I'm not sure how much longer I'll be able to resist.

At the same time, it feels like maybe he's right here with me.

Worse yet?

I'm pretty sure I don't want to resist.

CHAPTER THIRTY-ONE

Gruff

Andy opens the bathroom door and steam billows out ahead of her before she materializes in her pajamas.

I avert my eyes in a feeble effort to maintain my sanity.

"All yours. Sorry I steamed it up. The warm water felt so good."

She sounds relaxed and I refuse to look at her and take in the sight again.

It's already seared into my brain as it is.

"Thanks. I'll just be a few." I march in like I'm heading to a change of command, but my eyes are not up. They are down, practically on my feet. I slide into the bathroom and shut it behind me, breathing the scent of her soap and shampoo like I can live on the contact high for days if I just inhale enough of it now.

Good grief. I shouldn't know this smell this well. I'll be longing for it even more now.

I shower, enjoying the warm water for a few minutes before my mind takes a turn and I get out of there before any steamy thoughts about my wife can take over.

By the time I brush my teeth and exit the bathroom, she's snuggled up in bed with her ereader, a soft smile curving her lips.

My steps falter as I take in the sight. We've never shared a bed before, never shared a room, but we're married. And after the last few days, I feel this need to be close to her. I know we're not to the point of intimacy physically, but it feels like we're tiptoeing toward something more than what we originally agreed on.

"All warmed up now?"

Her words send me onward instead of hovering right outside the bathroom door. "Yes. Felt great."

I shuffle into the room like a lumbering beast. I don't know why but I feel particularly large in the space when she's cuddled into the bed and seems to be taking up so little room.

After dropping my worn clothes into a laundry bag I use for travel and rifling through various things in my backpack, I find my book and stoutly ignore the nervous energy thrumming in my veins.

I slide into bed on my side.

It's completely normal to be sharing a bed with one's wife, so why should this moment feel so... monumental?

It isn't. That's all.

Ah, ah, ah. But it is. Because she's your fake wife and you've never even kissed the woman.

All my best arguments screech to a halt when that unhelpful voice of wisdom blasts into my brain.

"I like this," Andy says, smiling over at me when I glance her way.

"What?" I croak. I wish I could say it sounded normal, but no, indeed. I croaked out the sound.

She hums a warm, pleased sounds that sends something hot snaking through my chest.

"Sitting here, reading together in the quiet. It's nice." She gives me one of those soft smiles I feel down to my toes, then turns back to her ereader.

Since my attention is already on her, I indulge in taking her in. She's got her hair braided and it hangs over one shoulder, her large T-shirt has some kind of illustrated cat on a sleigh ride, and her smile is ticking up again as she reads.

"What are you reading?" I ask because I have the sudden need to send a note to the author and thank him or her for their service. They've made her happy and she's just so damn beautiful when she's happy.

"Oh, it's a Christmas romcom about this woman who's running a Christmas village in her small town, and she needs help with constructing all the little booths and the only person available to help her is the hottie grump who's an expert at construction. So good." She wiggles her eyebrows. "What about you?"

I hold up the book so she can see the title. "It's a space opera. I don't read a lot of fiction but I try to enjoy it during Christmas and vacations. It's weird, I know, but just kind of how I've always been." There's a faint warmth at my cheeks which heightens when I realize it's a blush.

"I'm glad you do that for yourself. I'm of the persuasion that people should read what they want to read. If you like educating yourself and learning while you read, more power to you. And if I want to giggle and swoon and sigh and generally forget about reality, more power to me." She grins and winks one of her exaggerated giant winks.

I chuckle softly. "Agreed."

It's a simple thought—that people should read what they want to read. And yet, her stating it so plainly reminds me not everyone agrees. It's why I felt the faint blush rise to my cheeks as I admitted I read mostly non-fiction and some sci-fi, though I'm not sure which I was more tempted to feel embarrassment over.

What I keep discovering is that with Andy, I can just be me. She seems to like me decently well and any encouragement from her comes in some form of "keep being you, it'll be great."

It's odd and... lovely.

Perhaps this indicates my ego is out of whack and all I really want is to have someone who likes me. My ex never did, I suspect. But it's not that simplistic. I'm relieved and a bit amazed Andy seems to enjoy spending time with me but I look forward to being with her. In any room, my eyes are searching for her, and not just because that's what a husband *should* be doing with his new wife.

"It's why I'm contemplating including books at the café. It's a tough decision business-wise, but I'm considering making it a romance bookstore, too." She ducks her head. "Not that I'm anywhere near being ready for any of it."

My hand acts of its own accord, sliding over to her and grasping gently around her wrist. "You will be. You're prioritizing your health right now and that's going to allow you to do more going forward."

And I'll be with you every step of the way. The words were on the tip of my tongue, but I held back.

Will I?

Will I be there for any of it? Will she move out and be gone by the time she's ready to open her shop? Will she really be separated from my life entirely by the time she fulfills her dream?

An ache settles low in my chest, especially as her big, trusting eyes blink back at me.

"Your faith in me might be a bit misplaced but thank you."

"No, Andy. It's not. The only reason you're not living that dream *right now* is because of things beyond your control. That's not because you're not a hard worker or determined or prepared. It's because life happens and sometimes, we can't do it on our own." I will her to understand how much I admire her for being here with me, for what that represents to her. "You're being brave and taking care of yourself. I can't wait to walk into Feline Friends and Frappuccinos and marvel at your success."

She bursts out laughing, then covers her face with her hands. She's smothering the sound of her joy and I am sorely tempted to pull her hands away so I can see. When she finally looks back at me, her eyes are glistening, but she's smiling.

"Feline Friends and Frappuccinos is an amazing name." She beams, and I know it's not the actual name. She hasn't told me what it is and I want to ask now, but she continues, "I never would've believed you're this nice."

I scoff. "I'm not nice."

She shakes her head in slow motion. "Hate to break it to you, *husband*, but you really are."

I like the teasing lilt to her words, but I'm not sure I like that she's so wrong.

I'm not particularly nice. I'm certain no one in the history of my life has described me that way. "I suggested we marry for my own benefit. The fact that you get something out of it is just a bonus."

She huffs. "I see you've decided to be stubborn, and I suspect there's no going back now. I know the truth, even if you don't." She cups a hand to her mouth and stage whispers, "You're a sweetheart."

"You read too many romances," I say.

Her lips thin. "Impossible. Though I don't dispute it helps me be the positive, excellent person you know and love."

She coughs, eyes wide, and rushes to say, "I mean, not *love* love. You know what I mean. I know you don't love me. I just mean it like—"

"Calm down, woman. I know what you meant." But I also... could.

I could love her, and I know it vividly in this moment. The possibility is now bolded and underlined and not too far in the distance.

I have held my heart in a cage, wrapping it up behind bars so I didn't have to face the same brutal end I've experienced before. But Andy?

She didn't just walk in with a key. She almost instantly made me believe there was no need for the cage or the bars, and they're simply gone.

Her lips twitch and she nods. "'kay."

"Back to your book with you," I say, nodding at her ereader.

I focus on my book, but I can practically feel her smile when she says, "Yes, sir."

It's hours later, long after she sets aside her book and her breaths deepen, that I fall asleep with the full certainty that at least one thing she said tonight was right. And with the bars gone, it's up to her if she'd like to step in and *take*.

CHAPTER THIRTY-TWO

Andy

My internal alarm that has been trained by years of working early shifts at coffee shops alerts me to the impending morning far earlier than I would like, especially considering the late night we had.

I snuggle into the warm comforter and arch my back a little to stretch. I'll snooze a few more minutes and if I fall asleep in this cozy little nest, so be it. If not, I'll get up and explore what the early morning looks like at Maple Mountain.

Sighing, I curl closer into the warmth of the bed, then inhale the spicy-clean scent surrounding me, hand opening and tracing against a rather firm pillow. Lovely slopes and curves under soft fabric. The scent is delicious and masculine and—

I freeze and my eyes pop open.

Yes. Yes, the scent is masculine and the pillow is mighty firm because it is, in fact, a human man.

Not just any human man, though.

The grumpy-sweet man who married me to give me health insurance and refuses to believe he's a nice person. A man who indulged my idiotic notions of doing snow angels, then let me shower first despite him being utterly soaked through and freezing just like I was, and who is so ridiculously supportive it makes my head spin.

I am curled all up in his business and I mean *all up in there.* My butt is cradled in the crook of him, the big spoon to my little. I've been feeling up his shoulder and the curve of his bicep, full-on caressing him, huffing him, and I don't know if he's still sleeping or just staying super still but I must go.

I think I maybe even muttered something about how delicious he smells. I cringe because toward the end of my dream, as I was waking, I think I actually mumbled out something insane like, "Yummy."

My face is flaming and there is nothing to be done but move. Slow and steady, I inch away—one inch, two. Three inches—

A large, warm hand presses against my belly and there is a low, rumbly groan that melts my common sense and sets me on *fire.* His long fingers touch my skin because my oversized T-shirt I slept in has ridden up and I am aware of just how close we are.

We are so, so close.

And I do not hate it at alllll.

"Gruff," I manage to grit out. "I need to get up."

He groans again, sliding his hand up a few inches, and makes another sound that really shouldn't be legal in the circumstances.

I can't stay here, or he'll end up sliding his hand to any number of places, and we will never be able to come back from that. Or, even if he stays perfectly still, any more of this and I will melt into the sheets and never be found again.

Tearing myself away in a dramatic and very uncool move, I haul myself out of bed and don't look back to see whether he's awake or if those sounds were coming from a sleeping Will Gruff. I shut the door behind me and take gasping breaths like I've escaped a pirate on the high seas by the skin of my teeth.

Gruff as a pirate is not hard to envision. Just imagine—

I scrunch my eyes closed. "No. None of that." Cannot be imagining my fake husband as a sexy pirate.

Knowing I'd wake up first, I'd tucked my clothes for the morning into the bathroom last night before I fell asleep so I wouldn't risk waking him up too early rummaging around for an outfit. I'm dressed and slipping out as quietly as I can with brushed hair and teeth and a clean face in minutes. I snatch my ereader and a room key and tiptoe to the door.

Gruff is still a lump in the bed and the relief I feel cannot be quantified. It is buckets of reliefs. *Vats* of it.

Swimming pools of relief that have been covered and winterized. Skating rinks of relief frozen for all to twirl about upon.

But when I open the door, I hear his muffled voice. "See you at breakfast, Andy."

And I die.

Fine, I didn't die, but I did slink down the hallway and avoid eye contact with myself in the mirror of the elevator for fear I'd see me in a stunning tomato red mask of embarrassment thanks to the blush incinerating my face.

Who needs a facial peel when I can just burn off the top layer of my skin?

Once I get out, I find the lobby quiet save for one attendant at Reception. I'd spotted my destination last night, so I wander the luxurious halls until I enter the ski lodge's atrium room.

It's still dark outside and the huge windows that normally look out on the base of the ski resort are a dark wall of obsidian. If it weren't for the fireplace lit with bright flames, it might be creepy. There's also a huge Christmas tree towering to the right side all lit up in white lights, the red and gold baubles and balls reflecting their glow.

It's also very cold which probably means they haven't cranked up the heat yet, and I'm grateful for my oversized sweater and fleecy leggings. I'm not exactly resort chic right now, but I figure I'll change for the day after breakfast, anyway.

Despite the cold and darkness, to me, this is utterly perfect. The only thing that could make it better would be a peppermint mocha, but the coffee shop isn't open, and I probably shouldn't start on caffeine quite this early.

Okay, a peppermint mocha and my buddy cats. But they're getting daily visits and snuggles from Grace and JJ for now, and I'll be back to spoil them after Christmas.

I nestle into one of the overstuffed chairs facing the fireplace and sigh happily, blissfully ignoring the way I was snuggled up with Gruff not twenty minutes earlier, and I read.

Some amount of time later, awareness prickles at my

side, and I look up to find Gruff's handsome face staring at me.

"Okay, creepy." I say this like I somehow have the upper hand and not like I'm instantly disintegrating from the inside out with embarrassment at the groping I gave him this morning.

His eyes crinkle just a touch. "Didn't mean to disturb you. I was going to wait until you seemed like you were coming up for air but I've been here for a solid five minutes and you haven't so much as stretched."

"My Christmas romance is hitting the dark moment. I need to get my sweet characters to the other side, stat." But even as I say it, I'm uncurling from my chair, arching my back, and closing my ereader.

"How about we fuel you up with some breakfast and then you can get them taken care of?" he asks, extending a hand to me as he stands.

"Sounds good." I take what he's offering, my belly flipping at the contact. He's got objectively nice hands—warm and big and strong. I may have developed an unusual affinity for them based on the current flurry of butterfly activity in my chest at just this simple connection.

"Did you sleep well?"

My glance at his face reveals what I thought I heard—a cheeky little smile hovers there, barely visible.

"Surprisingly well. You?" Because I'm not about to be the one who breaks first. Heck no.

He's quiet as we navigate the hallways of the sprawling resort, slowing as we approach the location of the breakfast buffet. I think he's going to ignore me completely, but then he leans in and says, "Very well."

I catch a hint of his warm, fresh scent and my head swims with an unusual kind of intoxication. It's his fault, but I'm not sure why his straightforward response to my question feels so loaded.

Does he mean he slept so well because he was sleeping with me? Next to me? Woke curled around me, with me stroking his fabulously formed biceps?

It's this thought that has me humming instead of attempting words, and while I'm internally scrambling for something else to say besides an audible *squeee*, there's a rise of clinking coming from inside the restaurant.

I glance at Gruff and he gives me a similarly befuddled look right as Mrs. Gruff arrives with open arms and a giant smile.

"There they are! They're here, everyone!" She winks at me and gives Gruff a smile I'm certain he can read because his eyes widen and the curiosity and humor fall off his face like a boulder off a cliff.

My pulse instantly starts to climb, and I grip Gruff's hand more tightly like he can stop whatever is happening. People are rising from round tables seating eight or ten, no plates filled with food as though they've genuinely been waiting on us to arrive. They're standing, many of them using spoons and forks to *tink tink tink* against their water glasses.

I see Janie holding her spoon with a regretful droop to her wrist and the pleading look on her face sends my stomach to my toes right as Mrs. Gruff says, "Welcome to your wedding brunch, you two. Didn't think you'd escape a little celebration now, did you? Now go ahead and kiss the bride under the mistletoe—it's what they're all waiting for!"

I look up and sure enough. Right above where we've come to a stop is a cheery little sprig of mistletoe with a bright red ribbon so no one can miss it.

CHAPTER THIRTY-THREE

Gruff

The glint in my mother's eye is diabolical.

I shouldn't be surprised. Deep down, I'm probably not. Even so, I didn't anticipate this madness. I will be speaking to her about this nonsense at the earliest possible moment, but while every single eye in the room is on us and upwards of a few dozen family and friends await me kissing my new wife, I simply vow to have it out with the sneak, instead of acting on the need right this minute.

In the midst of our discussion about marriage being believable for my family, we didn't discuss physical contact beyond hand-holding. We wouldn't really need to perform in this manner, or so we naively believed.

Sweet summer children in a winter world.

A Christmas world, to be exact, because it's the mistletoe here that's going to be the reason we can't pretend with a quick peck on the cheek and call it good.

I look at Andy and find her bright, lovely eyes on me. She reads the words I can't say out loud—my insistence that if she doesn't want me to kiss her, I won't. We don't have to do this in front of a crowd or ever.

But she's nodding, not breaking eye contact. "It's okay," she whispers as softly as she can, her eyes flickering up to the mistletoe. I'm not sure I even hear it—I read her perfect lips.

Which I'm now looking at.

The jarring clinking of utensils on crystal has me wanting to end this madness as soon as possible, and she's given me the go-ahead, so I don't hesitate.

I cup her cheeks, send her a soft, and I hope reassuring, smile, and press my lips to hers.

On a barren island, life is found.

In a desert place, a natural spring rises up and trickles down over parched land.

An angel gets its wings.

A unicorn's sparkle brightens, and a leprechaun's rainbow doubles in size.

Or maybe the change isn't out in some undisclosed or fictional location, it's me.

I release her, distantly aware of polite clapping and a few hoots and hollers, and her eyes flutter open.

Yes, it's me. I am what has changed.

Despite being at times problematically private and perpetually wishing people would stay out of my business and life, I want to kiss her again.

Right here in front of everyone.

I want to take her rosebud mouth and devour her.

"Oh, wonderful. Now, you two go first through the buffet, and we'll all dive in!"

My mother is speaking as though I can make sense of

her words. She's talking like I want to move from this place where I'm still touching Andy in one of many ways I've thought about and like I have interest in croissants or bacon when I could kiss my wife again.

"That's so thoughtful," Andy says, her voice halting, but still kind as she turns her face to my mother.

Then I see her eyes dart to the side, and I register that maybe she's not feeling the moment like I am. She's not luxuriating in the points of contact and wishing we were alone so we could keep kissing without the garish tinkling of forks against water glasses or applause, like kissing in front of a room full of people under an actually poisonous plant is an accomplishment.

"Of course. I know the wedding wasn't..." My mother pauses for effect. She's aware this has come out of nowhere and she's not exactly saying she knows it's fake, but she's capitalizing on the fact that I don't want anyone to know it. She finds her words after a beat, continuing, "Something others were invited to, but we're finally all together now so I thought it'd be fun."

Fun.

Kissing Andy was something. Fun is one of many words I could use to describe it, though those three letters pale in comparison to the sonnets of words I'd need to use.

But I suspect she means fun for her—to watch me squirm, maybe see how Andy handles this, and Jason Gruff is absolutely relishing my dazed idiot brain. So I shake it off and guide Andy toward the buffet with a hand on her lower back.

"Thank you. I'm sorry if you were waiting on us a while —I assumed it wasn't a firm time so—"

"Nonsense. You couldn't have known. You're here now. Enjoy." She's off to check in on each table, the consummate hostess. We'll probably need to do the same at some point.

"Well, that was…" Andy tucks her lips between her teeth and makes a face.

"Bad?" I ask, revealing way too many of my cards.

Okay, it's not a poker game between us. I know this. I woke up to her stroking my biceps and sighing, so I know she's attracted to me on some level and likes me to some degree, too. Still, I'm not thrilled to reveal my fear of our first kiss being bad right here in front of the sausage patties.

Her expressive brows dip down. "I wouldn't have called it bad. I guess it felt like an ambush. And it was a surprise. But no." She bites her bottom lip before adding, "I would've said it was nice, barring the circumstances."

Nice.

She would call it nice.

I thought bad was bad, but now I know *nice* is worse.

A stupid thought, and yet, there it is.

I don't know anything right now other than my gut-level longing to kiss her again in a way that makes her redefine her vocabulary surrounding kissing me.

"You thought it was bad?" she asks, her tone casual as she scoops some decent-looking scrambled eggs onto her plate.

"I thought it was very public and unexpected and—" I cut myself off because my brain has, in the last three seconds, caught up with my mouth.

"And?" she prompts, squinting a little before she slides down the line and smiles at a man offering her a Belgian waffle.

The words are screaming to escape but I keep my jaw locked. It's not until we're through the line and we've taken a seat at a table where I saw Janie and Chip when we first entered, and they're now taking their turn at the buffet, that I give in to the gut-level need to tell her.

I lean my head down and whisper in her ear, knowing it's a foolish choice, a potentially damaging one, and yet unable to forget the soft slide of her hand over my skin this morning before she was fully awake, or the sharp intake of breath when our lips met minutes ago.

"I thought it was far too short."

Her fork pauses halfway to her mouth, and she blinks ahead, not turning toward me, not giving anything away until her lips purse together in a smile.

And suddenly, I'm not quite so irritated with my scheming mother.

M.O.M. NETWORK

Mothers Of Military Network Message board:

SCLDG: Oh yes. Yes. We are cooking with gas now.

CoolyKay: Oooooo.

Vic: Well, out with it?

JusticeLVR: Don't be a tease @SCLDG. What's the word?

SCLDG: Let's just say I learned a thing or two in my time. And never underestimate a little peer pressure and mistletoe.

CoolyKay: Oh my!

Vic: Ha. Schemer indeed, but I can't say I don't support it.

JusticeLVR: They have chemistry, then?

SCLDG: I saw more than one person fanning themselves in the wake of their kiss. If it wasn't their first, I'm at least certain it won't be their last.

CoolyKay: I love it.

JusticeLVR: You're a master.

Vic: Taking notes.

CHAPTER THIRTY-FOUR

Andy

Bliss finds me in the arms of a muscular yet surprisingly petite woman named Shannon, and I am ready to break my vows to Gruff—belief system, integrity, and general outlook on commitment be darned.

Okay, not really, but I did just have the most glorious ninety-minute hot stone massage and I am now wondering where they've been all my life.

Oh. Right. *Not in my budget.*

The women closest to the Gruffs are having a luxuriation day post-breakfast buffet while the men do... something? Honestly, I don't recall what it is because I've never had a true spa day and I couldn't be happier for my day's roster of events. I hope it goes okay for Gruff since the little I do know is that time with his brother, and especially with his brother *and* his dad, can be very difficult for him. I can only hope Chip has his back and that maybe the other people in attendance will provide a solid buffer.

Meanwhile, I'm lounging in the relaxation area between appointments. It's a large room with several cozy seating areas, a section of tiled heated loungers, and different rooms and showers and saunas we're welcome to use between treatments.

Don't mind if I do.

Simply put, it's divine, and the instrumental Christmas music and crackling fire at the far end of the space, combined with the subtle nods to the season with pine and cranberry flourishes here and there, is utterly blissful.

I'm soaking it all in and trying to remember if I have a facial or a pedicure next when Janie and Elaine emerge. Janie grins at me and I hold up the little electrolyte replacement drink Shannon gave me for an air toast. She raises her own small glass and winks.

"I swear these are the most delicious things on the planet after a massage." She takes a sip, then closes her eyes as she swallows.

"It does taste amazing. I've been sitting here half-conscious and also lowkey debating breaking my cell phone rule and searching up where to buy this stuff." I send another "cheers" to Janie and Elaine, who smile prettily, and sink back into the stone-tiled chaise. It doesn't seem like it'd be comfortable, but the little polished tiles are heated, and I feel like I want to lay on it naked.

But I won't do that because I'm not quite that comfortable with my body. Plus, it still feels great through the plush robe I'm wearing.

"Are you adjusting okay? Still jet-lagged?" Janie asks, and this is the chattiest she's been with Elaine that I've seen.

I'm proud of her. Not really sure what their beef is, but seems like a nice time to put it behind them.

Elaine finishes a drink of her own electrolyte tonic of wonders and smiles again, one hand on the round of her belly under her robe. "We stopped at my parents' house for a few days prior to coming to the lodge, so we're all adjusted fairly well. Takes a few days since Korea is thirteen hours ahead of US eastern time."

"Wow, that's a huge adjustment," I say. "I'm always amazed at expats because I've lived so few places." I'm currently the farthest away from home I've ever been so Korea seems... astounding.

Janie's smile flattens a touch.

Elaine glances at her, then says, "I had practice moving around before Korea, so that helped. Plus there's a huge contingent of Americans there between military and government workers."

"Oh, right. Well, that does help, I'm sure. I have so little interaction with military and government people despite living in DC my whole life." Well, just outside of, but that's an unnecessary distinction, and I'm feeling rather small. I'm a country bumpkin compared to this fabulously worldly woman.

Elaine is looking at me strangely. "Except Wilson, of course," she prompts.

Oh. Right. My soldier of more than twenty years husband... "Yeah. Yes. Of course. We're still relatively new and—" I'm not sure what else to say that won't make this more awkward or potentially reveal the eff word in our marriage situation.

Faux is the eff word, by the way. Get your mind out of the gutter.

"They're great together. Honestly, I love them together.

They are just adorable, and she really *knows* him in a way I don't think anyone ever has."

Janie's words warm me, even if she is in on the truth. But Elaine looks uncomfortable. I wonder if maybe she and Jason aren't doing so well?

Elaine's face is bright, probably falsely so. "That's great."

"Well, ladies. How are we? Relaxed to within an inch of our lives?" Mrs. Gruff arrives in a whirl of robe-covered glamour.

We all chuckle and I'm incredibly grateful for her arrival and the break in the odd tension. The knowledge I'm missing something is stronger than ever, but I'm not about to bring it up, especially not now that I know Mrs. Gruff is secretly an evil genius when it comes to getting what she wants.

This is my assumption, anyway, considering the Cheshire cat grin she was wielding the rest of the breakfast this morning. Our consequence for not inviting her to our tiny seven minutes-long wedding ceremony came under mistletoe at breakfast, and I am certain she didn't tell us so we had no time to prepare.

Everyone chats about how wonderful their spa services were and then we're each off to more pampering. It's more solitary than I imagined save these brief communal moments, so I've got time to think about Gruff's words whispered softly, but with an edge of determination, and the way my heart took off at a gallop the second his breath curled around the shell of my ear.

Or the moment when our lips met.

It wasn't a complex kiss and it was oh so very public, but it only made me want more from him.

By four that afternoon, I've been massaged and facialed

and pedicured and steamed and everything one can imagine, so much I'm restless for fresh air and conversation with Gruff. I haven't seen him all day, and while I enjoyed the spa, the longer time ticked away, the more concerned I became that the group dynamic of Gruff men would not ultimately be a good thing.

I get showered and dressed and there's still no sign of the man. We're supposed to meet for an "après ski cocktail hour" and then everyone is on their own for dinner again, thankfully. I gear up for more small talk with people I don't know but who know my husband very well, and head downstairs, my pulse skittering with anticipation of seeing the guy I haven't stopped thinking about since I woke up stroking his biceps.

When I arrive at the designated location for the après ski, I find a charmingly casual vibe of people in jeans, boots, and warm sweaters, and others still in their ski clothes. I spot Gruff talking with Jason and Elaine and make my way there, realizing he must've spent his day skiing based on his attire.

It's not until I arrive and set a hand on Gruff's arm that I realize this isn't a happy chat they're having. There's strain on everyone's faces, and the tension radiating through my fake husband is palpable even in the most basic contact.

"Hey, how was your day?" I ask, though the tone says something more like, "Are you okay?"

Jason looks at me and grins. "We had a great time skiing. Did you ladies enjoy the spa?"

He's all charm and thousand-watt smile. I can see how he might charm people he's wooing on behalf of the United States, though I never really imagined diplomacy to be about charm. Maybe that just shows how little I know about it.

"It was lovely. I am thoroughly relaxed," I say, smiling up at Gruff only to find his stern expression unmoved.

Jason rushes in again. "Well, sorry to steal him away right when you arrive, but I need just a minute with my brother."

Gruff's expression remains unchanged. *Okay.* I don't know what's going on, but it's not really my place to keep him from talking with the brother he's spent the entire day with, is it? Should I be shielding him? I don't think so, though I wish his expression would give me *something*.

"Sure. I'll just be here," I say, and turn to Elaine so I seem fully capable. I'm wishing I knew more people, or that Janie was here. I like Elaine well enough, but our conversation earlier felt a little off and I'm definitely not oblivious to the odd tone of the little chat circle I invaded moments ago.

"So you two have been married for..." Elaine's eyes shoot past me to where Gruff must be.

I turn to see him standing silently while his brother gesticulates. A pulse of anxiety slips through me, and I see him raise a hand to his temple and press.

Worry streaks through me. Is he getting a migraine?

"Oh, uh, one month today, actually." I didn't realize it until right now.

"Very new."

She says this like it explains something, and I don't know why it shoots irritation straight to the fore, but it does.

"Yeah," is all I manage because I nearly say, "What is your problem?" Thankfully, I hold in that rather confrontational question.

"But you're happy? With him?" Elaine asks, clearly oblivious to my rising frustration with her.

Something about her disbelieving tone has me ready to abandon all pretense of being socially acceptable.

"I just mean, he's only going to continue the same way he always has... I don't know that I could've done it for much longer. I hope it's..." She fades off.

I am stuttering, stumbling, absolutely fumbling for words. "You—you couldn't do what much longer?"

She shakes her head, eyes definitely on Gruff again when she says, "Stay married to Wilson."

And, oh.

There it is.

The thing I've suspected—something hidden I knew I was missing but Gruff refused to tell me. The truth I've been utterly blind to and am now slapped across the face with.

Elaine is Will's ex-wife.

She divorced him.

And married his brother.

CHAPTER THIRTY-FIVE

Gruff

I see when it happens, too far away to interject or stop
the trainwreck.

Andy turns, her mouth open just shy of agape, and her
blue eyes find mine. All I can think is *should have told her;
should have told her; should have told her.* Why didn't I just
tell her the truth? Why did I wait for her to find out in
public when she couldn't process it with me, or even *at* me,
if she felt she needed?

Because you're a coward.

Lightning strikes in my brain, a sharp whip of pain
behind my right eye and a clear harbinger of what I've
known was coming since about two this afternoon. Between
the stress, the altitude, and the changed routine, I almost
have no choice but to face a migraine here.

Problem is, I have no time for it. I see Andy say something to Elaine, who seems genuinely surprised by Andy's upset, and then my wife is speed-walking out of the restaurant. She brushes past Janie, grasping my cousin's arm and apologizing even as she keeps moving.

Finally, my feet unglue and I'm going after her.

"Better move quick, dum dum," Janie helpfully says under her breath.

I don't call out for Andy because I want to find somewhere quiet to talk to her. She's shoved out a side door and is leaving boot prints in the two inches of fluffy snow that have fallen late in the day.

"Andy." There aren't many people out here but enough that I draw their attention. Andy must not hear me, though, because she keeps going, down a set of stairs and through a small courtyard.

"Andy, wait!" I yell now, anxiety that she'll ignore me and just keep plowing ahead gripping my heart and my head at once.

She doesn't, though. She turns and I'm not sure what I expected, but she's almost stoic when she sees me. "What?"

There's no sharpness to it, no anger. I was expecting a fight—a scene of epic proportions, and she's giving me hardly anything.

"I'm sorry." It's the most important thing.

She nods. "Me, too."

"Why are you sorry?" She doesn't flee as I close the distance between us. "This is my fault."

She's shaking her head, her face pained. "I guess I'm sorry in two ways. First, that you didn't feel you could tell me. But I think I might understand why."

My heart is beating in my throat as shame and embarrassment, and the tiniest hint of relief, flutters in my chest. "You do?"

She presses her lips together and clears her throat. "I can't imagine what it must be like."

There's a sink hole in my sternum. The bottom drops out and the edges disintegrate and soon it's a gaping wound I haven't let myself acknowledge fully. But it's not like before. It's not the reality I faced three years ago when my ex-wife married my little brother. It's the knowledge that Andy knows the truth now, and she'll never see me the same way again.

"It's not great," I admit, because saying anything else feels like far too much.

She huffs out a laugh. "No. I can't imagine so."

She's hugging herself, holding onto any body heat she has because the sun has dropped below the horizon, the stars are winking at us again, and it's brutally cold as the wind whips past.

But before I can offer my jacket, she launches into my arms. "I'm so sorry."

I hug her back, tucking her into the sides of my coat, and close my eyes as her freezing hands hold my neck and pull me to her. I am a split between ecstasy with her contact and despair that it's *this* drawing us together.

"You have nothing to be sorry for. *I'm* sorry. I should've told you so you'd be prepared." I don't want to excuse myself, but I have to. I can't make her think it's her. "I didn't want to explain that my ex-wife is now my sister-in-law. It's humiliating and at the same time, part of me doesn't care. It's this messed up back and forth and I hate thinking about it. I didn't want to spend any of our time together explaining it because sometimes, I don't understand it myself."

She pulls back but keeps her hands on me, pressed into my chest like she's giving me strength and taking some of my warmth. I keep the edges of my coat wrapped around her and think maybe this is how I'd always like to stand if I'm outside in the winter.

"How can you not care? I want to go in there and scream in their faces and I tend to be fairly easy going. I mean... what? I don't even... like, how? How did they ever think getting together was okay let alone—" She shakes her head. "I don't know exactly why you and Elaine split but it's just..." She makes a disgusted *ugh* sound.

Maybe it makes me a terrible person, but I laugh. She's not the first one to express disgust at the situation—I know she's not. My mother navigated it far more diplomatically, of course, but Janie and Chip both gave them a pretty hard time, and it wasn't until I asked them to bring it down that they let up.

There's something about Andy being furious about it that makes me happy. It's wrong, I'm sure of it, but I like that she's bothered and mad at them instead of pitying me. Damn, but it feels like a genuine relief, frankly.

"I think it's because Elaine and I were never right. I did love her, especially at first, but we were ham and peanut butter."

She gives me a stricken look. "Um, ew."

I chuckle, internally marveling at the way I'm laughing in a moment I have been dreading for as long as I've anticipated it. "Exactly. Both solid sandwich ingredients but not together."

"Never," she says, and shudders, inching closer to me.

I shake my head, smiling so wide it's ridiculous. "Right. And we didn't know that. I messed up, and she messed up. And yes, it does feel bad that she's married to my brother sometimes. But she also really loves him, and he loves her. They fit together in a way that she and I never did. He's her cheese."

A frozen cloud escapes from her with a breathy laugh. "Yikes."

I shake my head again and practically laugh. I feel so light right now. "Right?"

She's grinning at me and I'm more than a little devastated by this moment. Because it's too good. And she's so calm and happy and it's nothing like I feared. It's so much better and I know it has nothing to do with where I am in all of this. It's because of her—her goodness, kindness, and friendship.

Maybe it is me a little. Or rather, the way I feel about her.

Because this entire trip, I've been less worried about how my family would treat me and more consumed with how they'll treat her. But now that she knows the truth about the family dynamics, I'm set free, especially seeing the lack of pity for me.

I don't have to fear her finding out anymore. She knows the truth and she doesn't see me as a failure, as less, or as somehow pitiable. She simply knows me better, knows the things I've been ashamed of, and she... well, I don't know how she feels but it's not less than before.

I ask her what I don't want to voice, but what I think we need to do. "Are you up for going back?"

She looks into my eyes so deeply I worry I've misread every second of this. Her eyes are glittering in the moonlight and she's still close enough for me to almost feel her chest brush against mine. There's this hesitation hanging between us, like she wants to say something, but she doesn't.

"Of course. Let's do it." She backs away and tucks her arms around herself.

I shrug out of my jacket and drape it over her shoulders.

I might hear a little gasp, but then she's smiling over her shoulder at me.

"Like I told you. You're a sweetheart."

We walk back inside and when we're through the doors, she hands me the jacket. I take it, then slip my hand into hers. She grins and I'm certain I'll never get tired of making her smile.

As we enter the lighted hallway, I feel the pressure in my head growing, like the removal of all that dread has loosed the small elves to hammer away at my brain matter, no holds barred. If I were a smart man, I'd go straight to the room, take meds, and put myself to bed. I'd pray to the migraine gods to spare me from the worst of it.

Maybe it's pride urging me onward into the room full of people who know all my dirty laundry and witnessed my own wife learning the truth.

"Want a drink?" I ask, steering her to a high-top table with stools where we have a nice view of the sky. The yurt-style room has glass on all sides with blond wood and white fur pillows and a very Austrian look. It reminds me of a few places I've visited over the years in Europe.

"Uh, sure. Maybe just a hot chocolate?"

I nod, then raise our hands and press a kiss to the back of hers. "Be right back."

Despite the dramatic reveal I've dreaded and the looming headache and the general discomfort of being in a room full of people, I'm eager to return to Andy where she's smiling softly while people-watching those around her.

I cannot wait to simply stand next to her and know that she *knows* me. She's seen me, even the truths I didn't want her to know, and she's still here, smiling, letting me be near her.

If everything else that's happened today doesn't tell me enough, I know it with that observation.

I love this woman and there's nothing I wouldn't do for her.

CHAPTER THIRTY-SIX

Andy

Since the bar isn't closed to the Gruff family Christmas extravaganza gathering, it's gotten crowded. Will has been gone for more than a few minutes and I can see there's still another person in front of him before he'll be able to place his order.

I want to tell him to bag it, but I suspect he needs something to do. And as much as I hate to admit it, I need a minute, too.

I'm relieved to know the truth and I'm also gutted by it. It feels so ugly to acknowledge, but I am drowning in the sensation that I have very little in common with anyone here. Not that I was under the illusion I did before, and I'd made peace with that, but now?

I don't know why knowing Elaine is Will's ex is tipping me over but it is. I hate that I care or feel anything other than mild disgust with her and Jason for getting together, but I do.

I also can't stop thinking, "I'll be your jelly!" and wondering if he chose to classify himself as peanut butter knowing how deeply I love a PB and J. It's nonsense I'm stuck on this, but I can't help my mental wandering down that deliciously salty-sweet-creamy-nutty path.

"So you really had no idea Elaine was my brother's ex, huh?" Speaking of, Jason sets a beer on the table next to me and is giving me a big, charming grin.

And yet, the words are anything but charming.

"Well, we're pretty—"

"I've been trying to figure out why my paragon of honor big brother would marry a woman but lie to her about his past, and I think I've figured it out." He's squinting at me now like he's figured *everything* out.

His head bobs down and I register he's talking a little louder or more pointedly than I've heard him before. His eyes tell me this isn't his first or third beer.

"He didn't lie to me, he—"

"I think," Jason begins, slow and confident in a way that only a man who is used to having power over other people can, "that this whole thing is a sham."

I freeze. No breath in, no breath out. It's like he's a predator and I'm the prey hiding in the bushes, convinced this monster won't see me if I don't move.

But he does see me. He can tell I've lost my footing, and I have no idea how to respond, because he plows ahead.

"Is he paying you? Are you some kind of escort? A call girl maybe?" He dips his head. "I don't indulge personally, but he's got good taste. You're down to earth—real natural-looking."

He slides a finger along my wrist, and I am seized by so

much horror and fear and disbelief I cannot think. I cannot summon words of any kind and I have no idea what to do, so I just stand here, a deer caught in this creep's tractor beam.

"You can tell me, you know. I'm sure you've got a contract and everything's by the book. That's the way he'd do it. I may think it's pathetic he couldn't find a real spouse, but I have to give him credit where it's due. He chose well, and if he made sure to loop in the physical benefits, then—"

"Step away from my wife."

The words come in the closest thing to a growl I've ever heard issue from a human. Will is instantly at my side, standing between me and his brother.

"*Wife*, is it? Are you sure?" Jason's sneering now.

Will takes him by the collar. It feels like he's moving in slow motion, or maybe the world around us is frozen. When he hauls his brother close to his face, it's with a snarl as he says, "Don't speak to my wife again. Don't look at her. Don't stand within ten feet of her."

There's no *or else*, and at a core level, I recognize it's because a man like Will Gruff doesn't threaten people. Instinctively, I know that if he were going to punch his jerk of a brother, he would just do it. He wouldn't give him a big speech.

Will turns to me. "You okay?"

I nod once, stunned by... everything that happened in the span of maybe three minutes.

"Let's go." He slides an arm around my back and we're walking. I'm unaware of everything around us, my attention zeroed in on the warm arm pressed to my upper back and a low hum of something welling up in me.

I don't pay attention to the route we take, only the way my heart is still racing despite Jason being nowhere in sight.

He accused me of being an escort? He knows it's fake between us?

Is it that clear? Can people really tell just by looking? And how is this something I'm hung up on right now?

By the time we reach the room, I'm so tired I can hardly think. In fact, I'm not thinking at all. I'm not trying to understand the over-full feeling in my chest nor am I debriefing with Will over the events of the last ten minutes. I'm just... blank.

"I don't know how you'll ever forgive me." His voice is low and the defeat in his tone is audible enough to force me from the haze of exhaustion I'm in.

"There's nothing to forgive." I squeeze his hand then release it. "I'm just going to go to bed."

His gaze ensnares me, and I wish I was up for discussing what just happened. I can't tell whether it's everything that's happened or something else, but I can hardly hold my head up.

He nods. "Of course. I'll see you in the morning."

I move through the motions of getting ready for bed as quickly as possible, and when I sink into the soft covers on my side, I don't even attempt to read.

I wake with an emotional hangover so acute I wonder if this is what a migraine is. I sit up slowly and marvel at the fact that I didn't cry a single tear and yet I feel swollen and bruised like I spent the whole night sobbing into my pillow.

Next to me, the bed is empty. The *room* is empty. And

Will's suitcase is standing up near the love seat, not sitting open on the luggage rack.

Before I get too discombobulated, the door opens and he arrives with a coffee in one hand that he instantly brings to me. He sits with one hip on the bed near my knees. "Sleep okay?"

"Uh, yeah." I can't explain why I feel runover by a truck, so I just don't mention it.

His intense gaze is flitting over my face, from what must be a rat's nest of hair to my eyes, cheeks, lips, and down. "Good. We're leaving in an hour."

My mouth drops open. "What?"

He is so serious and stern, it feels like he's angry with me, but I'm not in a weak enough state to get confused about that. I know where his anger is directed.

"I'm not going to ask you to stay in a place where you've been disrespected. I won't do it."

The reality of my total shut down last night comes crashing into me at this moment and I set the coffee aside so I can grab onto his hands with both of mine. "Please don't do that. It's... I don't know. It's giving up. Letting them win. I admit I was thrown by all of that yesterday but I'm fine."

His brow turns down even further. "There's nothing to be gained by staying here."

Panic hits me in a sideswipe. I'm not sure why, but I sense that if we leave now, it's not just the trip that'll end. I suspect that the unfinished business here will mean *we* end and I'm waking up knowing with remarkable clarity I do not want that to happen.

I'm upset about what Jason said but the lingering feeling I can't shake is the fact that he knew it was fake. How could he know? Is he just a suspicious jerk? Because it has felt so, so real to me and the fact that he called it out makes me feel nothing less than heartbroken, if it's a reflection of the way we're headed.

I don't want that. I don't want heartbreak for me, but more than that, I don't want to lose Will, especially not to some comments his idiot brother made. The thought cements the reality I can't ignore anymore—nothing is worth losing Will. Not his brother's inebriated mistake, not my pride or fear of wanting more out of this than our original agreement, and not even, I hope, his insistence that he'd never marry for love again.

Because that's what this is. It's love. It's been building since the day he found me on the street and no amount of playing pretend or ignoring the truth will stop my heart from beating double-time now that I've made the connection.

I love Wilson Gruff.

"Maybe not. But we could also stay and just... have fun." It's not the right argument, but it's something. I need more time to help him see we could work and we can't leave now, just when we've got all our cards on the table and have truly started to get close. We can't end this because of his stupid brother.

I need him to see this is possible and maybe, just maybe, catch up to me.

A knock at the door has him narrowing his eyes. "One sec."

He answers the door and keeps his voice low enough I'm not sure who's there, but then he says, "Mother—" and Mrs. Gruff herself is storming into the room.

She rushes to me, and I am horrified to realize she's seeing me with ratty hair and a puffy face and my faded Grinch T-shirt.

"My dear, I'm so deeply sorry for my youngest son's behavior. Janie told me what was said, and I am aghast."

Who says aghast in real life? This woman. But the veracity in her tone is unmissable and the way her soft hands grip mine tells me she is genuinely horrified. She's still perfectly put together in nice jeans and a sweater and gold, subtle earrings and light makeup that make her look polished but casual, but she's strained around the eyes and her grasp is firm enough to say she won't let go until I hear her out.

"I'll admit it's not every day I get called a call girl."

Her mouth drops open but then she laughs bold and loud. "Too true." She glances over her shoulder at her oldest son who is standing like a storm cloud on the horizon with arms crossed and brow furrowed the most it has ever been furrowed.

It's quite a lot of furrowing, really.

"I understand completely if you feel you need to go." She dips her chin and pins me with her gaze. "But I hope, lovely Andy, that you will consider staying."

My eyes jump to Will, then back to her.

"I will do everything possible to keep everyone in separate places. You can feel free to skip any planned events. But I hate for you two to miss out on time together without the distractions of DC. You've made it all the way here, after all, and it's only another two nights." She turns and presumably gives Gruff a pleading look because his gaze hardens in a way that tells me he's resisting something.

"I'm fine to stay. Truly. If Will is willing to stay, then so am I."

Mrs. Gruff grins, then rushes to her son. "Wilson James, I will—"

"Save your bribery, Mother. We'll stay."

She jumps a little, clasping her hands. "Wonderful. I'm truly delighted, and I promise everything will be perfect from here on out."

She sends me a wink. I would get out of bed but I am wearing my Grinch T-shirt and some bright red undies and nothing else because I was so whooped last night, I didn't even think about someone seeing me like this, so that feels more unseemly than not getting up.

Mrs. Gruff is back to business, bustling toward the door with a little finger twiddle as she goes. "Okay, enjoy your morning. The ice-skating rink opens soon, and they're doing sledding, too. If you feel like making me a grandbaby, you'll certainly make the holiday even better."

I gasp and Will coughs. Mrs. Gruff pops back into view. "Love you both." With one more wink, she slips out and I turn to share a moment with the man still frozen in place in the middle of the room.

"She really just said that, right?"

He nods, still looking toward the door. "She's a master."

I chuckle, less horrified and more amazed at the way she navigated from making amends and begging us to stay all the way to us providing a grandchild.

He takes a big breath and his shoulders sag. I sink back into the pillows and laugh to myself. When my eyes open, he's staring at me with an expression I can't read. His gaze is caught on my bare shoulder where my T-shirt has slipped down, then it jumps to my thighs where the comforter has fallen away.

He clears his throat, and his eyes bounce to mine. "Sledding?"

"Sounds great."

I get moving and try not to think about what a mess I'm in.

Gruff

I think I'm losing my mind.

Andy is sitting between my legs on a two-person tube-style sled and it is heaven. Normally, I don't think I'd be quite so obsessed with the position we're in, but I haven't stopped thirsting after nearness with her since I had it the first time, and it's only getting worse.

I can smell the pepperminty scent of her shampoo. When she glances behind at me and asks, "Ready?" I am transfixed by her lips.

And when we begin the slide down the wide lane of the sledding hill, the chilly winter air pummeling us in the face as we whizz past onlookers and skiers on the other side of a fence separating us from the ski hill, I feel light.

That might be the air we're getting as we launch off a small jump. I'm holding onto the handles of this sled in a death grip and Andy is giggling—yes, giggling. She's effusive in her experience of everything and this is no different.

And this is what I want.

This wild woman who is soft, but so strong, and is currently holding on with one hand and has the other thrown into the air, hollering with so much joy I can practically taste it. The tube is her bull and she's getting her full eight seconds.

She is who I want.

As we come bouncing into the end of the course, my heart is racing like our crossing the finish line is a matter of life and death, but I know the adrenaline is only partly from our sledding run.

The other is this realization. Because I'm a man who appreciates clarity and vision, and once I have it, I move forward with determination.

What I want—what I'm even now planning to do as she tumbles out of the inner tube and laughs at herself, then reaches out a hand to me—is counter to everything we've agreed on.

"Are you okay in there?" she asks, peeking at me like I've disappeared into a cave.

Fair enough, since my realization and the subsequent part-glee, part-panic response is still driving the mental train.

"Yes. I'm good. Just wondering if I'll ever recover from your braid whipping me in the face." *Lie.*

I love it. If I'd been willing to release my death grip on the handles, I would've had a perfect excuse to grab hold of it. For now, that action remains on my personal bucket list.

She yanks on my hand, and I get my feet under me, feeling remarkably brittle as I rise to my full height and my knees creak.

"You going to make it there, Colonel?"

I shoot her a well-deserved glare.

She grins.

And good grief, she's pretty.

I shake my head and snatch the sled from her. She's capable of dragging it but she's still favoring her good wrist, especially in the cold, and there's no sense in her getting hurt when I can do it just as easily.

"Wanna go again?" she asks, literally skipping along next to me.

"I think I need something to eat."

I never ate breakfast in my whirlwind planning attack this morning. I spent the night thinking over everything my brother had done, everything I'd been bracing against, and by the time five a.m. rolled around, I was calling the airline to rebook us. My migraine has held off thanks to furious hydrating and the moderate painkillers I used instead of the big tranqs I need when its full-blown.

Discovering Andy doesn't hate me and my entire family this morning has undoubtedly helped, as well.

Maybe my launch into leaving Vermont seemed impulsive, but Andy's response to Jason's idiotic and cruel words scared me. I'd never seen her like that—numb and locked out of her emotions. Usually, she overtly exemplified whatever she was feeling—happy, excited, energized, sad, angry... she wears her emotions on her sleeve like a gold star. And though I'd only seen her in the "sad" state one time in earnest, even that had been so fully alive and pure.

I still don't know whether she simply wanted to avoid talking about what Jason said or if something more was happening. She certainly seemed incapable of discussing it by the time we got back to the room. Shoulders slouching and eyes were drooping, she was in a full system shutdown.

This morning she seemed better, but in the wake of my mother suggesting we whip up a grandchild for her, we've avoided any more serious conversation.

But the way my heart feels like it's pounding out of my chest in an effort to get closer to her?

I need a minute before I straddle her again.

"I could eat," she says, her eyes bright.

What is it about this woman? How is she so deeply, intrinsically... sunny. She's got this light radiating out of her, this willingness to be in the moment and enjoy what's around her that I just don't have.

Except being with her makes me want to do better. In fact, I already am. I've *enjoyed* more days in the last month since we've been married than I have in the previous five years combined. That's both a pathetic reality of my own life before her and a testament to her at the same time.

We each take a handle of the sled and begin dragging it toward the large conveyor belt carrying them back up the hill. In the corner of my mind, I hear an uptick in noise that sounds like yelling. It's only when I glance up the hill and see a sled barreling down, coming right for us, that I jump on instinct.

In a move less like a heroic rescue and more like a messy tackle, I grab Andy around the waist and fling us both as far out of the way of the sled as possible. Curling around her when we land, I hear her small *oof* on impact.

Behind us, I hear, "Dude, you saved her," and other people clapping, so we must be in the clear. I look down to find her gazing up at me with a stunned but appreciative expression.

"Are you okay? They must've gone too soon. We should've been clear of the bottom before they got going."

I'll be having a word with the person at the top, though I'm certain the staff at the bottom has already radioed for them.

"I'm fine."

Her voice is strained and I'm instantly on alert.

"What's wrong? Is it your head? Your spine? Are you—"

"You're kind of crushing me," she wheezes out.

And then I realize it.

I am actually crushing her. The full weight of my lower half is on hers and the way I'm leaning up over her is likely placing more pressure on her diaphragm. I push up, removing myself in an instant.

"I'm so sorry. Are you hurt? I—"

Her gloved hand on my cheek halts me.

"I'm fine, Will. And I'm much better now than if we'd gotten plowed into by that sled."

She's got one of her soft smiles going that makes me feel a little dreamy and things I can't say are on the tip of my tongue.

"Good. Still sorry, but good."

She shakes her head, the smile widening with each movement. "No apologies for being my hero, okay?"

I don't let myself dwell on her calling me her hero. I'm not a particularly heroic man. I'm a decent one, I can admit, but the entire context of her being here is self-serving. And I'll do well to remember that.

CHAPTER THIRTY-EIGHT

Andy

Our waiter delivers a refill on our fries and sets our burgers in front of us. We're back at the brasserie location for lunch, and I am delighted to be facing down this burger topped with Boursin cheese and fried onions. It's indulgent and precisely what my tangle of feelings demands.

"That looks good, too," I say, eying the "breakfast burger" Will ordered which features a fried egg and bacon.

"It is, though I'm sure it's a terrible idea for my arteries." He makes an exaggeratedly alarmed face I can only see as adorable because months ago, he never would've done this in front of me.

We are seeing each other in new ways by the second and I am loving it. I'm gobbling it up like this burger, which I've already consumed almost half of in mere minutes. I guess I was hungrier than I realized.

"You seem like you're in pretty good shape for your age." My eyes blow wide when I register my words. *You need to finish that other half of your burger before you speak, woman!*

Will's brows raise and he finishes chewing a bite. "For my age. Interesting."

"No, not interesting. You look great for *any* age. Babies probably envy you your supple skin and—"

"Andy, honey, I'm joking."

That *honey* zips straight through me. "Oh, right." I smile at him, feeling all kinds of soft and mushy about him. "But really, you're super good-looking and fit and I am not just saying that. You're like," I make a gesture indicating my mind is blown.

"I am *mind-blowing?*" His disbelief rings clear. "You're going to give me a big head."

My cheeks are burning but I'm laughing. "Oh, I don't think you can blame me for that. You've got plenty of confidence. But you are definitely handsome."

His grin is so boyish, I want to kiss him.

Crap. Don't think about kissing him!

"You have to stop looking at me like that, okay?" I laugh because he's too ridiculous. It's like he's never gotten a compliment before. Really? *This* man? He might be stern and a bit grumbly and stiff, but he's flat out good-looking and I dare say that's objective. "Can we just pretend those comments were all part of my après-ski haze?"

His smile drops away. "Can we talk about that?"

I take a giant bite of my burger and chew with zero hurry, but eventually, I swallow and nod my agreement. "In retrospect, I think the events of the day caught up with me, but I'm also feeling pretty worn down. My body's dragging a bit, especially later in the day, and by the time we got to the room last night, I just crashed."

His serious gaze is back, boring into me like he can see through my skull and right into my brain. "I'm sorry. I haven't been giving you enough time to rest, and—"

"No. Will. This is not on you. I've been dealing with these symptoms for months and I'm still working on how to rest. Plus yesterday, I spent the bulk of the day getting massaged... in most scenarios, that would count as rest."

He tsks. "Maybe, but you were with my family, and you found out about Elaine, and then Jason..." He shakes his head with a sneer. "I can't believe he said what he did. We don't get along, but he's never been like that."

I hesitate, but ultimately end up admitting my suspicion. "I think maybe he was a bit tipsy. And I don't think over-indulging is an excuse to talk to someone the way he did me, but it does help explain it a little."

He still looks furious, so I add, "Please, let's not worry about that. I don't want to think about it anymore."

After reaching for his water, he agrees. "Fine. Can we talk about your surgery?"

Nerves roll around in my belly. "Sure. It's January seventh. Should be a few hours between checking in and the surgery itself and recovery, assuming everything goes well."

"Which it will."

"Right. And then assuming I'm doing well after, I can go home that night. They may decide to keep me, but my doctor seems to think if all goes well, I can choose to go home." I think of the bedroom at his house and my silly cats who are likely going a little stir-crazy, though Grace is checking in on them.

"Good."

"Grace will be there with me the whole day and she'll bring me back, but she did mention I can stay with her and Justin if that's best." My cheeks flame anew because we haven't discussed this.

He stiffens. "Absolutely not. I'll be there with you, and I'll bring you home to your house so you can recover in your room in your bed. Period."

Our eyes are locked together, his dark gaze so intense and his tone so certain and forceful I am... stunned.

Relieved.

More than a little pleased by this outburst and bossiness because it gives me the hint I've wanted.

I may be having too many thoughts about how much I like Wilson Gruff, but he's not immune to me, either. A whole fleet of butterflies—no, sugarplum fairies and snowflakes—are fluttering around in my chest.

"Yes, sir," I finally say.

He scowls.

"Wilson, good," Mr. Gruff says. "I'd like you to meet me in the salon in the east wing in an hour. I'm rounding up your brother and we'll have a quick chat."

Mr. Gruff hardly acknowledges me, though he doesn't really engage with Will beyond giving him an expectant tilt of his brows before he pats our table and walks away, Will still looking on in silence.

"That sounds fun," I offer weakly, already dreading the encounter on his behalf.

"Should be a blast."

He doesn't say another word about it, though. We keep chatting as we finish lunch talking more about the pretty lodge and the stories about PB and RJ Grace has sent than the looming meeting his father so lovingly invited him to.

When we've finished, he pays the bill, and we waddle

away from the table having stuffed ourselves to the point of discomfort. He holds my hand gently but in a way that tells me he's not letting go. It's not tentative or apologetic. It's insistent, and I love it.

He freshens up in our room, changing his shirt from the waffle knit Henley that did lovely things for him into a button up. I wonder if this is like putting on armor, or a requirement to even walk in the door.

Before he leaves, he bends and places a kiss on my cheek. "Come get me in half an hour?"

And I know it's not just for fun. It's a potential rescue mission.

"I'll be there."

CHAPTER THIRTY-NINE

Will

My father sits in a high-backed leather chair like he owns the small bar set at the far end of the resort. I'm sure he feels he owns it, having rented out so much of the place over the course of these few days. Nothing is ever as simple as showing up for him, even now that he's out of actively serving as a senator.

The temptation to tug at my collar is vivid and I see myself doing it, but years of self-discipline keep my hands at my side as I walk. I'm furious to be summoned like this to a meeting with my sniveling brother, and I'm preemptively exhausted with whatever this is. He's also already touching the edge of his glass to my brother's, a medium brown, clear liquid swirling in each crystal high ball vessel.

I am so full of the late lunch Andy and I just finished, even thinking about drinking Scotch makes me feel ill, never mind that drinking hard alcohol is an insta-trigger for migraines for me when I'm already on the verge. I've been skirting the line and have miraculously avoided one, but if any interaction has the power to bring one on, it'll be this.

"Wilson, good." He turns to me and nods to the chair at his left.

Jason shifts in his seat and avoids eye contact with me. *Nice try, buddy.*

If he thinks he's going to get away with not acknowledging the idiocy he pulled yesterday, he is sorely mistaken.

"What's this about?" I ask as I sit, internally bracing against what I suspect is already coming.

"We're having a little meeting. Just making sure everyone's on the same page." His meaningful look lands on Jason, who glances up in time to catch it.

My brother clears his throat and shifts again, then slugs back his whiskey. I'm startled to realize he's taking this down like a shot and not the undoubtedly ridiculously expensive sipping whiskey my father ordered us. I'd offer him mine, but I don't think it's a good idea for him to keep throwing them back.

"You know all about me, Dad, so no need to belabor it." His gaze cuts to mine, then away again.

Shifty as all get out, and I'm not about to let him off the hook. "Oh, no. Let's do. I want the full update. You know I don't get much between visits."

My mother knows I don't particularly want to discuss him, and my father doesn't usually discuss him when he's centered his sights on me. All in all, I genuinely have very little awareness of Jason and Elaine and whatever it is they're up to.

Jason's head ducks low and I realize there's something wrong. Not just Jason being a little twit like usual.

"J, what's going on?" I ask, hoping my tone conveys

concern and not the same *gotcha* sentiment I felt seconds ago.

It's my father who speaks first. "Your brother is moving back to the US. He's ending his time playing around at the embassy and transitioning out of diplomatic work." His mouth tilts up, so he's not altogether upset about this.

"Ah. What's next, then?" I can barely find these words because I'm stunned. My father has always made it a point to demonstrate the excellence of Jason's career trajectory. But it was always in the context of... *oh.* "Wait, are you planning to run for office?"

Jason's head is bobbing lightly. "Yep. Time to continue the family legacy. First me and later you, right, Willy?"

When our eyes meet, I finally see the watery misery there. I might've begrudged him what I thought was our father's favor, but it's like I've got the wool torn from my eyes and I get it now. It was never favor. It was always a matter of comparison—to each other, to him, to what we *should* be doing if we're going to live up to the illustrious family name.

As though either of us is a failure.

"Congratulations, if that's what you want," I say carefully, vowing to find a time to talk with him alone. He needs a little bit of the freedom I've always insisted on, much to my father's genuine dismay.

"And you? When can I expect my first-born to take his place in politics?"

I sigh and decide not to respond. If I had a nickel for every time....

"You'll need to annul your marriage, but I suspect you know that. I'm not sure what you expected us to believe when you brought her here, but she's not the kind of woman who flourishes in the political life."

My stomach knots and I go from irritated and concerned for my brother to furious in a split second. The energy generated from my rage could power the next rocket to the moon. My hands fist in my lap and my jaw clenches. All I need to do is wait him out. Let him have his say and then I'll leave. Box checked and back to the life I'm making for myself that isn't cowing to some fictional version of life he has in mind.

"You're past the point of retiring now, aren't you? It's time, no?"

My father asks this like he doesn't know. The man forgets nothing, and especially not the point at which I could walk away from my military career. That I have stayed in for several more years is continually baffling to him.

My choosing to do anything other than exactly what he says has perpetually been a source of frustration. He only allowed for my time in the military because there are, in fact, some constituents who like to see someone with military experience. Heck, he might even imagine me to be someone who could run for president someday, and wouldn't it be handy if I'd survived a war or two?

I can't stay quiet now, though, because he's asked me a question that is less rhetorical and something that might be worth directly responding to, unlike his garbage comments about Andy.

"I can retire any time, but I don't know what else I'd do. In fact, I've just come up on orders for an early summer move."

"Oh."

My head whips around to find Andy a few feet away, her eyes wide.

"Sorry, you said to come find you. I'm so sorry to interrupt." She backs out of the place, then bolts. She's literally running away and my heart rockets to my throat as does a searing clarity that *this* is the time to set everything straight.

I'll find Andy and fix things between us, whatever's just broken based on what she overheard, but it's long past time I make myself known to my father and let him choose how he wants to proceed instead of refusing to be honest and attempting to avoid the family drama.

I stand and pin my father with a look I hope he will see as veracious and determined. "I love that woman and I intend to keep her. I'll do whatever I want regarding my career and when I get out of the military, I will not transition into politics because I have no interest in it. It doesn't mean I don't respect you for what you gave to the country, how you served, but it won't be the same for me. The sooner you embrace that, and my wife, the better."

I stalk away but turn back and hook my brother's gaze. "And you need to grow a backbone and do what *you* want. Talk to Elaine. Talk to *Mom*. Talk to people who care about you and know what you're good at. Be done in SK if you're done, but don't leave because you need his approval. If he can't see you for who you are, then he doesn't." I turn, but reverse course one last time. "And when you apologize to my wife, you better mean it."

And with that, I leave, fury and fear riding at my heels as I race to find Andy.

CHAPTER FORTY

Andy

It's not that I'm completely shocked by anything I just overheard. It's more that I'm surprised how much it hurts.

The cold air slices at me as I burst through the doors to the outside. Considering we were just here a few hours ago, it's shockingly cold. The sun is gone, though, and a layer of gray gloom has descended, almost like the sky planned to match my mood.

I don't want to be this person running away from her problems, but I couldn't very well stay and confront Mr. Gruff or Will. I intruded on their private meeting. It didn't matter that Will had told me to.

"Andy!"

His voice reaches me right as I hit the edge of a plaza. I'm in unknown territory on this end of the resort and I have no idea where to go. I just know I can't let him see the tears freezing on my cheeks. I can't let him know what I'm feeling.

He's got orders. Which means he's leaving. *Early summer.*

This isn't a surprise. He told me this was coming. I've been a fool to think all of this was leading somewhere important. I've been an idiot to let myself open up to the possibility of more.

"Please don't keep running. It's a sheet of ice out here and I don't want you getting hurt."

Will's warm hand is on my arm, and I swear I can feel the heat through the layer of my sweatshirt. Yet again, I have failed to dress properly for the frigid Vermont winter, but I hadn't anticipated going outside.

"I'm not running," I protest, finally turning to face him fully.

"You literally were. I had to run just to keep up and I have ten inches on you." He's scowling at me but there's a softness in his eyes I can't miss.

"Irrelevant since I wasn't running."

His hands slot into his hair and he looks around, pacing away until he blurts, "You are so stubborn!"

It's an outburst that bounces off the stone pavers underfoot and startles me. He's genuinely frustrated with me, and my insides shrivel even more.

"I'm sorry. I shouldn't have been there. I didn't mean to hear what your dad said or that you have orders. That's all private and I shouldn't have been there."

He stalks back to me and takes me by the shoulders. It's the most demanding he's ever been.

"My father is an arrogant, classist jerk sometimes and he has one thing on his mind at all times. He wants to continue what he calls the *Gruff Political Dynasty* and I hope you know by now that is not what I want for my life. His opinions about you are based solely on *that* and have nothing to do with who you actually are or how *I* feel about you."

Direct and definitive as usual, but I am still shooketh. Because it is exactly what I needed to hear—at least regarding his dad.

"Okay. Yeah."

"I hope you don't let him change anything about what we're doing because he doesn't matter. I love him, he's my dad, but he's not the person who decides who I am, what I do with my life, or who I love."

His dark eyes are pinning me in place, and despite the cold, I am thawing.

The freezing fear that had me running, it's cracked through by the shock of what he's hinting at, and sure enough, I can feel my fingers and my toes.

No, I'm not just thawing, I am *melting*.

Who I love.

It echoes through me, and every bit of my tender little heart reaches out with needy fingers and grabs at the words, begging to claim them.

"Right. Of course. I get that. My parents don't even know I'm married."

He blinks. "I guess I can't be shocked about that since I haven't met them. It was always supposed to be—"

"—temporary." We say it together.

We both know.

There is another thought waiting in the wings, though. Both of us feel the gigantic snow-covered *but* on our lips, and I beg him to be brave enough to be the first to say it.

"But I'm not sure about that anymore."

My brave Will Gruff, he *is* the first.

"What does that mean, you're not sure?" I ask, because I'm bruised enough right now, I'm not brave yet.

His hands slide up to my neck and I startle because they are *ice*. "Holy crap, can we please move this inside? We're both freezing."

He laughs, his handsome face lighting up and he gets this hazy look, then grabs my hand and is literally running with me toward the building. We make it in seconds, tucked inside, and then pacing a few feet down the hallway from the entrance so we don't feel any of the cold air.

"Better?" he asks, furiously rubbing his hands together to warm them, then cupping them and blowing warm breath into them.

I nod, charmed by his urgency.

"Good, so, where was I?" He inches closer and settles his still-chilly hands on my waist.

"I think you were about to say something important..."

One of his dark brows arches. "Indeed. But first..." He hauls me close and wraps me in a hug so delicious, I could live off it for months.

He smells so good, like cinnamon and mint and cold air and himself. And his large, long arms have me wrapped up completely. He's leaning down and holding me close enough my head is resting on his shoulder and my lips are an inch from his neck.

He pulls back before I indulge the heart-deep yearning to press a kiss to that sensitive skin.

"Thank you," he says, voice a little graveled.

"Thank *you*. Nice *and* an excellent hugger."

His lips purse, but I see the smile he's hiding before he sobers and slips his hands down my arms to take my still-chilled fingers in his.

"The last month has been the best of my life. I didn't

plan this arrangement with anything other than both of us getting what we want out of it. But I feel like what we both want has shifted."

I nod, heart fluttering so hard I can hardly stand up.

"I don't want to end this just because you've recovered. And I don't want to walk away just because I don't need a wife anymore." He shakes his head like the idea is preposterous. "Need isn't the point. It's *want* now. *Choose*."

"What about your orders? You have to move, right? I mean, I don't want to have to end this either, but I can't—"

"You can't leave Alexandria. I know that. Because by this time next year, your cat café, Andy's Animals and Affogatos, is going to be the premium destination for cat café and book lovers this side of the Mississippi."

I laugh at his ridiculous name, but my heart is aching.

"So where does that leave us?" My voice thins with the emotion clogging up my throat.

"Andy, honey, I know I'm not easy to read, but I love you. I'm in love with you. It's probably too fast but for me, it's so clear, I can't escape it. And I don't want to. I've never felt like this before and I'm not giving that up for a job."

I am speechless. My mouth is hanging open and I want to kiss him and scream at him at the same time.

"I literally just said I can't move because of *my* job." It's a stupid response, but it's real. I feel awful for being so inflexible.

"No, you can't move because of your *dream*. That is completely different. And for me, I'm at the end of my military career. I've been looking for a reason to start the next phase of my working life—to get out of the Army and see what else I can do."

I swallow hard. "And I'm the reason?"

He chuckles low. "I worry that if I say yes, you're going

to start running again. I'm not trying to pressure you. I just want you to know that if you want me, I want you. If you need more time, that's fine, too. I can wait." His brow furrows, and his head drops lower. "It may sound hokey, but I think I've been waiting for you my whole life."

I can't take it another second. I pull out of his grasp and take his head in my hands and kiss him.

CHAPTER FORTY-ONE

Will

Andy's kiss is just like her. It's heartfelt and joyful and better than Christmas morning.

She is soulful and generous in the give and take of her kiss. And this isn't in front of an audience, nor is it fleeting like our first. Because as soon as her lips hit mine, I knew I wanted more—as much as she would give.

I slide my hands into her hair, that glorious hair I've wanted to touch, and tilt her head, deepening the kiss and reveling in the way she melts into me further. It's unbelievable this is only the second time our lips have met. She is new and alluring but familiar and so damn precious to me.

Her mouth opens and our connection locks into a give and take I'm consumed by. It's life-giving and soul-stealing in one breath. Every piece of me wants this woman, and this kiss is just the beginning.

Her hitching breath. Her taste. *Her.*

Everything between us has been a slow burn, a subtle but inevitable cascade into what bursts inside me, a wildfire now.

Heat blazes through me from the tips of my fingers where they slip from her hair against her neck, up my arms and spiraling into my chest.

It's only when I register that we're still standing in the resort hallway I pull away, not wanting to share this part of our story with anyone else.

When I inch back, she has fresh tears tracking down her face. I wipe them away with my thumbs, cradling her face.

"What is this? More tears? Am I that bad at kissing?"

As I hoped, a watery laugh escapes. "I think based on the way I was oblivious to the world around us, you know you're not bad at kissing." She smiles wider now, then sniffles and steps back to wipe her eyes.

I give her a moment, wanting my hands back on her but understanding me crowding her won't help her say what she needs to say.

Her lips tremble but she firms them. "I'm worried that if you give up your career, you'll resent me. And as much as I want more with you, I can't take that. I won't."

"I would feel the same way. I would. But I need you to believe me when I say I'm done with the Army. I mentioned it last week and it's not new. I was already questioning my desire to take another assignment, but I've gone along with the process due to inertia. I even told you about how tired I've been, how uninterested in work despite enjoying my colleagues. I don't want to move again. I don't want to leave my house and have to rent it out or pay Janie to come water my plants. And I don't want to leave you."

She still seems pained by this, like I'm sacrificing too

much, so I try to explain it in another way. But first, I take her hand, sliding our fingers together in an intimate hold.

"I haven't laughed like I have with you. I haven't *enjoyed* life like I have since you entered it. Even before we were together, even when I thought of you as this irritating person my best friend's wife associated with, you drew me in. And having known you, seeing the way you treat your friends, customers, me, even your cats... it's only drawn me more to you."

"I want to believe you," she says just above a whisper.

"Then do. And also wait and see. Be with me and let me show you how grateful I am for you. Let me take care of you after your surgery and when you're exhausted in the weeks after you open your shop and when you're sick and when you're old. Please let me do that—let me love you."

She sigh-laughs and shakes her head. "How am I supposed to say no to that?"

I grin, my smile so big, it must be eating my face. "You're not."

Her beaming smile answers my own. "Well, alright then. I say yes."

"You'll settle for me? Trust me and give this a shot?" I'm all hope.

She cups my face in her now-warm hands, palms scraping against the short beard that's grown in the last few days. "Being with you isn't settling, Will. I had no idea what a deal I was getting when I married you for the insurance."

We laugh together and glance around, fakely concerned about people hearing. But we're alone in this hallway, this moment, and my heart is so full it could burst.

"You are kind and loving and smart and so darn sexy, it kills me." She bites her lip and her eyes dip to my lips.

Pretty sure my entire body lights on fire. "That is one

aspect of marriage we have definitely not properly explored."

"Something to remedy, if we're serious about this being more than our original arrangement." She holds out her hand, a pleased look on her face. "I'm all in."

I couldn't be happier to agree. "Me, too."

Despite the desire to toss her over my shoulder and run back to our room, we agreed that as much as we want to explore the new parameters of our relationship, it *is* a sudden shift. We've changed all the rules, and we're still here in this resort with what feels like everyone I've ever known, though it's really only a few dozen relatives and close friends.

Instead, we go ice skating. Though frigid, once we're properly outfitted in snow pants, jackets, gloves, and hats, swirling around on the rink is actually fun.

"I never would've imagined you'd be a graceful skater," Andy says, showing her own familiarity with the sport by doing a small twirl.

"I played a few seasons of hockey when I was growing up." I race toward her and stop, spraying her with the scraped-up ice.

She laughs. "You know I'm only in this for the post-skate hot chocolate, right?" She glances over her shoulder and flicks her braid for emphasis.

I finally do what I've wanted to and grab onto that braid —gently, and right as she's watching. She grins.

I die.

Well, okay, not really. But I could die a happy man like this—just here, with her, knowing she's not restless to get rid of me after her surgery.

"What's that look?" she asks, head tilting to one side.

"I'm just basking in your glow."

She bursts out with a laugh. "My *glow*?"

"Yes. You're just so lovely and joyful. And I don't mean that you can't feel other ways—there's no pressure from me ever. You're wonderful, and I'm grateful to be here with you."

Pressing her lips together, she steers herself back toward me and we collide. "Closet sweetheart. That's all there is to it."

She kisses me until someone hollers the most original *Get a room!* And we break away, a little embarrassed but not really.

Mostly just happy. And amazed. And shockingly glad we came to this family vacation.

CHAPTER FORTY-TWO

Andy

We're sitting on the couch at Will's house with cats sleeping on either side of us. RJ must've missed us enough that when we returned, he adopted Will into his pack and now he accepts nothing less than a headbutt every few hours in loyalty pledge.

We returned last night after our four nights in Vermont just in time to snuggle up in front of the fire with the blissed-out cats and fall asleep watching Christmas movies. It was perfect. Especially when Will carried me to bed, and we celebrated in new and very fun ways.

"I have one more gift," he says, sliding off the couch and disappearing down the hallway.

PB raises his head, then snuggles back down when he realizes no threats are in view.

"Where's he going? He already gave me too many

presents." I'm a woman with so many gifts, I don't know when he had time to buy them.

They're not all costly, but they're all lovely. A special edition of my favorite romance author's whole set, a framed photo of me and Grace at her wedding last summer, a small pendant necklace with a cat sitting on a book and it is the cheesiest, cutest thing I've ever seen. He also bought me a new winter jacket when he found out I didn't have one I really love, and gave me a giant gift card to our local bookstore. It's an embarrassment of riches.

I did my best for him, but honestly, it all feels fairly slim compared to everything he's given me. He loved the vintage books from a British General I found, and he genuinely seemed to love the "Cat Dad" shirt I got him. Silly things, but I guess they mean something, even when they're small, if you've given enough thought to them.

He returns and is holding something behind his back. I expect a cheeky expression or something playful based on the way he's hiding it, but when I see his face, it's anxious.

I push up from where I've slumped over, eying him. "Everything okay?"

He nods and abruptly shoves a manilla envelope at me.

"This is your last present. But I have a few caveats first."

I'm staring at the envelope like it'll announce its contents.

"Okayyy." I draw out the word because my mind is running, trying to guess what's inside.

"You are not obligated to do this. But I thought it might be a—a nice gesture." He cringes, grumpy with his own word choice. "Calling it a present was the wrong thing. Can we strike that? Can we pretend I didn't say that?"

I set a hand on his knee to calm him, hoping my touch

will reassure him. "We can. And whatever this is, if you let me see it, I promise I'll listen to you explain it if need be."

He nods at the *nice gesture* and I get the message, pulling the papers out from inside the unsealed envelope. *Termination of Formal Agreement between Wilson J. Gruff and—*

"Is this divorce papers?"

His eyes go wide. "No. Absolutely not. It is the document to end the agreement we made indicating we'll stay married until after the surgery and all that. If you see the next document, it's a post-nuptial agreement that basically says you get half of everything of mine, I get nothing of yours, I can't take the shop or any future businesses from you, and—"

"That hardly seems fair." I'm annoyed, but also ridiculously pleased.

"We can negotiate later. The point is you don't have to do this. We can keep the arrangement in place until after your surgery if you want. You don't have to worry."

Everything in me softens as I look at him worrying over how I'll feel about this. I cup his face and slide the fuzzy edge of his Santa hat back so it's not covering any of his handsomeness. "I'm not worried. I trust you, and I love this idea. It's a new phase for us. The perfect present to ourselves."

He nods, smiling now.

"Merry Christmas, Mrs. Gruff."

"Merry Christmas, Will."

CHAPTER FORTY-THREE

Will

Two Months Later

Having gone to war a time or two (or six, but who's counting?), I often get caught up in thinking I'm inured to the stressors of everyday life.

It's a completely false notion, but it helps me to cope when I do feel stress, especially acute versions of it. Sometimes, it helps shift it a step or two away from my body—like the difference between standing next to a fire and being consumed by it. I still feel the heat, might even get burned, but I won't be killed.

It's this thought I cling to through Andy's surgery. She's been so brave as she's gone through the waiting for this day, which has been moved three times due to the surgeon getting sick and an OR scheduling conflict, steps of pre-op prep, and now.

Now, she should be about finished. She should be out and heading to recovery and the doctor will come tell me it went perfect, and everything is perfect, and my wife will still be herself when she wakes up.

I don't know why I need to reassure myself this is what's about to happen, but it's that fear I pretend I've mastered creeping in. It's having had a taste of a life more beautiful than I ever could've imagined, and now facing a very real-world danger. Do most people die during this relatively minor surgery? No.

Do some?

Yes.

And that is enough of a chance for me to feel the anxiety hardening in my gut and taking up residence in my chest. I've been genuinely strong and hopeful and positive about all of this because I have every reason to be, and it's helpful for her if I'm confident and positive.

But inside, I've been shaking. We've had an incredible couple months together—celebrated Christmas, New Year's, and the first Valentine's Day I didn't hate. I've declined taking new orders and have submitted my retirement packet—this time next year, I'll be out of the Army. It's a huge change but one I've never felt more ready for, especially with Andy by my side.

I've fallen more in love with her by the day, but I've been genuinely fearful that just as I've found her, the love of my life, I could lose her. These changes are almost too good, aren't they? Can I really expect to be this happy, this hopeful, and keep it?

"Mr. Gruff?"

I jump up out of my seat and rush to the woman who just spoke my name.

"Yes? That's me. I'm Gruff. Wilson Gruff, Andy's husband." There is no masking the nerves seeping into my words.

"Your wife is in recovery now. A nurse will come get you in just a few minutes." She continues, sharing a few details about the surgery's findings, which are all as expected, and leaves me to wait a while longer.

I thank her profusely, then practically stumble back into the chair I just vacated.

"You made it. Take a deep breath, Gruff." Grace pats my shoulder and shoots off a text, presumably to JJ, who'll be waiting to hear.

"Thank God. I'm not sure I've ever been more nervous." I swallow hard, knowing no one will ever know how true the statement is.

"No reason to fear, but I get it. When you've got a glimpse of life with your person, it's hard to face anything that might interrupt that." Grace smiles softly at me.

"Exactly.

Andy

Will enters my hospital room with a gigantic bouquet of flowers. He sets it down and rushes to me, but stops just before he reaches the hospital bed, eyes a little red-rimmed and hair wild. He's been running his hands through it, clearly stressed, and I think I fall a little more in love with him.

It's not that I'm glad he's been worried. It's just another glimpse of that tender heart of his. It's so beautiful, and I'm deeply grateful he's here.

"Grace is right outside but they didn't want to have both of us and overwhelm you. You know my mother is texting every three minutes with grand-cat updates and to know when she can visit."

It's like he needs to apologize—like somehow, he imagines I'm disappointed he's here, or that his mom is obsessed with her grand-kitties and, funny enough, me.

I reach for him, grasping his warm hand and urging him closer. "Thank you for being here. I know waiting can't have been easy." My throat is a little sore, voice a bit rough from being intubated, but it's a relief knowing this part is over. I don't say anything about his mom—he'll keep her posted and I give her an hour before she shows up with flowers.

He chuckles, but it's gusty with relief. "I didn't love it."

I chuckle, too, feeling the pull at my neck. I hope the incision doesn't freak me out, or him. I hope it heals up okay. But knowing the doctor's happy with the outcome, I'm not going to complain. I'm just ready to feel better and move on.

"I love you," I say, the emotion welling up and running over.

He takes a seat on the bed next to me and reaches up, stroking the hair out of my eyes. "I love you. Thank you for letting me be here."

He leans in slowly and presses the softest, sweetest kiss to my lips. It's a dream and something I never had the creativity to dream up. I'm so glad life is better than what I imagined.

"I have something for you, if you want. It can wait, though."

He's still working out his nerves, his hands a little shaky where he holds mine.

"I'm always happy to accept presents, surprises, gifts, tributes…"

He smiles, then pulls a small envelope from his pocket. "For you."

I squint at it as though I have X-ray vision. "Don't tell me this is another amendment to our agreement or something…"

He just shakes his head. "Open it."

I fumble around with it, wincing a touch at the creepy feeling of my IV in my arm. I'm a baby about that internally but don't say anything. Inside the envelope is a check for—

"What?! That's insane. Will, no." I'm gaping at him because the number on this check is outrageous and it's his signature at the bottom. I've gotten to know the look of it in the last few months and this doesn't compute.

"It's not insane. It's actually a very reasonable amount of money for an investment in a small business, from what I'm told."

I blink at him, eyes welling with tears and so acutely overwhelmed, I'm scared I'll crumple completely. "But you can't."

"Andy, honey, I can. If you can wrap your head around it, I want to be your investor. One of them, at least. I want to help you get your dream off the ground. I want one of every single weird cat shirt you design, and I want to watch people fall in love with Andy Gruff's Gatos and Grandes."

That gets me. "Worst one yet." I chuckle and swipe at the tears on one side.

He's holding my other hand, so with his free one he reaches up and runs his thumb over the other cheek. "Let me do this with you. Support you. We'll draw up a contract or whatever you need to feel good about it. I just want to—"

I kiss him. When I pull away, I sink back into the pillow. "Okay." I peck his lips one more time. "But we'll have to discuss this again because I'm not sure how much I'm going to retain today."

He winces. "I should've waited. I'm sorry."

I cup his cheek. "Don't be sorry for being excited to support me. It's part of who you are. I love that."

"I love you," he says, gray-blue eyes shining at me in the harsh glow of the hospital lighting.

"I love you, too."

EPILOGUE

Will

Ten Months Later

Andy is the most gorgeous human being I've ever seen.
"Are you going to help me, or just keep staring?"
she asks, tapping her foot impatiently from inside the front
doors of her store. "The cats are going to be restless."

The cats. One might assume she means PB and RJ, but
what she's actually referring to—*whom*, I should say—are
the fourteen cats waiting to be released into the meeting
room at the cat café part of Andy's Place, Cats, Books,
Coffee.

Sadly, she didn't take any of my suggested names.

I slip through the bright pink door she's propped open

and press a kiss to her cheek. She's beaming at me, and I can't help but steal a real kiss now.

"Hey, we open in like half an hour. Can you get a little urgent with me, Will?" She flashes her brows up and down, then wanders to the check-out desk and register in the far corner of the entrance area.

The building is old, but the space has been thoroughly renovated. Downstairs, she does food, books, and coffee. Upstairs are the cats. I'd imagined it all smashed together with tufts of cat fur drifting on sunbeams into unsuspecting coffee mugs, and corners of books gnawed into submission by a cat simply asserting himself.

Alas. The separation of cat and coffee has proven to be a lovely combination, and also allows for a far broader clientele since those who don't want to mingle with cats can simply not pay to play.

"Did I hear you say Janie asked you to call her?" she asks, rustling around behind the desk.

I straighten the chairs we were too lazy to deal with last night after the Christmas party we held here for staff and friends of the café. It's why we're opening late today, and why Andy's worried about the fourteen cats who live upstairs. They will not be happy to have waited so long for their morning greetings.

"She said she had news—I don't recall if she gave me a hint about it, though. Maybe something about someone named Corbin? Colin? Something." I was in a haze of morning bliss after Andy woke me up with her usual energy, enthusiasm, and wifely attentions. I won't say more than that, but a text from my beloved cousin didn't quite puncture the fog.

At least it wasn't Jason, who apologized profusely and

more than once in the last year since working through his own issues with our dad and in his own mind. It has been healing for all of us in a way, and I'm grateful he's done the work for himself and been brave enough to face me and, most importantly, Andy. She forgave him before he'd groveled enough, in my opinion, but that's just who she is, too big-hearted.

But he definitely wouldn't have gotten through, either.

"The idea that Corbin and Colin are names you could mix up is amazing." She's shaking her head.

"Is it? They're both c names. Both c-o names that end in n." I stand triumphant, then deflate. "It's your fault. Those little Christmas tree pajamas you wore..." I shake my head.

Her cheeks brighten and she skips over to me—that's right, she skips. I didn't realize how much of her bursting energy had been hampered by her health issues until after her surgery when she'd fully recovered. Then she started doing things like skipping, running, jogging, jumping, cartwheeling down the street, and it was completely bonkers.

Good grief, I love her.

"Well, I won't apologize for those. Plus, my husband bought them for me." She settles her hands on my pecs.

I grasp her delicate wrists. "Smart man."

She grins. "Smart. Kind. A sweetheart, really, and rather talented with his—"

The doorbell jingles and a FedEx driver arrives with a package for Andy to sign for. She does so and forgets all about whatever sweet nothing she was whispering to me in favor of plunking down the box and tearing it open. Then she pulls out a bright pink T.

"I love it. Do you love it? Try it on!"

And that's how I end up wearing a bubblegum pink T-shirt with a hand-drawn cat holding a sign that proudly suggests the viewer "Come for the coffee, stay for the cats" at Andy's Place. This is her most popular shirt, though it's one of several designs, but this iteration features a little Christmas hat tilted jauntily over one of the triangular ears and a garland necklace.

Ridiculous. But fun and joyful and indicative of the cheery lightness visitors can expect from the shop itself and its owner, as well.

We unload the Ts onto a table and she gets to work folding. We've discovered my folding skills and hers don't mesh.

In the last thirteen or so months, we've learned a lot about the parts of us that do and don't fit perfectly. There are many things that click, a handful that don't—like my folding, which she finds nonsensical, and I maintain is absolutely logical—and all of it is part of what we enjoy about each other.

Maybe it's because we started where we did with an agreement and no plans to fall in love, but this time around for me feels so vastly different than my first marriage. And it's not like this relationship with Andy is just good *in comparison*. No, it is good, full stop. It is often great. It is sometimes hard. It is genuinely beautiful and brings me so much joy, and I feel more anticipation for the years stretching ahead of me than ever before.

Even if I spend many of them in shirts covered with cats.

Thank you for reading Andy and Gruff's story. If you missed JJ and Grace, read it in I'll Be Married for Christmas. Or hop over and read all about Gruff's favorite ski resort, Silver Ridge Resort, in The Silver Ridge Resort Series.

AUTHOR'S NOTE AND ACKNOWLEDGMENTS

Thank you for reading another military marriage of convenience Christmas romcom! I'm so happy to have Gruff and Andy's story on the page. I loved writing these two sweeties.

Is Wilson Gruff a touch young to be a jaded Colonel? Eh, maybe. If you've been around long enough, you've met soldiers and family members with incredible stories. I hope you were able to suspend your disbelief that a man in his early-ish forties had that o6 locked in.

This book is releasing at a time when my husband has hit a new milestone in his military career and we've just celebrated his promotion. So I want to say thank you to him for his twenty-plus years of military service and for being a man who has his priorities in line. Thank you, Matthew, for your incredible and perpetual support of me and our family while you serve our country in a way very, very few people do. Here's to finishing this part of our journey well, however long that takes ;)

Thank you so much to Genny Carrick for the early read and thoughts, to Zee Monodee for her insightful developmental edits, and to Jamie McGillen Editing for her thorough proof and feedback. I appreciate you so much!

Huge thank you to Maureen C., an awesome reader and member of my FB group, for naming this book!

Huge thank you to ARC readers, bookstagrammers, booktokkers, Facebook group members, and newsletter subscribers for celebrating this Christmassy book. I wish we could all grab a coffee and croissant at Andy's Place and then go snuggle some kitties.

Thanks to you for reading Andy and Gruff's story. I truly appreciate you for spending time in this little slice of the Claire Cain catalogue. Happy Holidays and Merry Christmas, friends.

ABOUT THE AUTHOR

Claire Cain lives to eat and drink her way around the globe with her traveling soldier and three kids, but is perhaps even happier hunkered down at home in a pair of sweatpants and slippers using any free moment she has to read and cook. Or talk—she really likes to talk. She has become an expert at packing too many dishes in too few cabinets and making houses into homes from Utah to Germany and many places in between. She's a proud Army wife and is frankly just really happy to be here.

You can also join Claire's facebook reader group for exclusive content and fun: https://www.facebook.com/groups/clairecain/

Website: http://www.clairecainwriter.com

E-mail: Claire@ClaireCainWriter.com

Newsletter sign-up for new releases, exclusives, and freebies, including a free book:

http://www.clairecainwriter.com/newsletter

a amazon.com/author/clairecain

BB bookbub.com/authors/claire-cain

O instagram.com/clairecainwriter

f facebook.com/clairecainwriter

g goodreads.com/clairecainwriter

P pinterest.com/clairecainwriter

J tiktok.com/@clairecainwriter